Agent McIntyre wasn't motivated by love, but rather by duty.

He'd stay over Krista's garage and unravel this threat before anyone got hurt. She sensed he was a warrior type, a controlling force.

Krista turned off the lights and headed upstairs. She didn't want a controlling force in her life. She'd fought long and hard for her independence.

The past was the past, long gone, buried with the news that her father's killer had died in prison.

It had been years since the nightmare had resurfaced to haunt Krista. Yet tonight, thanks to a stranger breaking in to her house and the DEA agent sleeping in her garage, the violence was back in her life.

Along with the memories.

HOPE WHITE

An eternal optimist, Hope White was born and raised in the Midwest. She began spinning tales of intrigue and adventure when she was in grade school, and wrote her first book when she was eleven—a thriller that ended with a mysterious phone call the reader never heard!

She and her college sweetheart have been married for thirty years and are blessed with two wonderful sons, two feisty cats and a bossy border collie.

When not dreaming up inspirational tales, Hope enjoys hiking, sipping tea with friends and going to the movies. She loves to hear from readers: hopewhitebooks@gmail.com.

Hidden
in Shadows

HOPE WHITE

Steeple
Hill®

Published by Steeple Hill Books™

STEEPLE HILL BOOKS

Steeple Hill®

Recycling programs for this product may not exist in your area.

ISBN-13: 978-0-373-67440-4

HIDDEN IN SHADOWS

www.SteepleHill.com

Printed in U.S.A.

Though a mighty army surrounds me, my heart
will not be afraid. Even if I am attacked,
I will remain confident.
                                    —*Psalms* 27:3

This book is dedicated to my friends at
Sassy Teahouse in Redmond, Washington.

ONE

Okay, so Krista didn't expect a welcoming party when she returned home from her mission trip, but she didn't expect the house to be trashed either.

As she stepped inside the front hallway of her bungalow, a shaft of moonlight illuminated the mess in her living room. Sofa cushions were strewn across the shag rug, the end table was tipped over and mail littered the floor.

Anastasia was not happy. Who would have thought a ten-pound cat could actually do so much damage? That she could tip over furniture?

Krista dropped her purse, went to the oak bureau and pulled the chain on the vintage lamp.

Nothing.

"Anastasia," Krista scolded. The cat had probably chewed through the cord again. You'd think one shocking experience would be enough for kitty to keep her fangs off the electrical wire.

"Come on, Natalie took care of you." Krista edged her way through the living room, hoping to find a lamp with an unchewed cord, and hoping she got some light before her attack cat decided to pounce.

She tried a second lamp, with no luck. Being stalked by a crazy cat in broad daylight is one thing, but in pitch black it could be its own kind of shocking experience.

"Kitty, kitty, kitty," she cooed.

Krista was so not in the mood for surprises. Exhaustion filled every cell of her body after spending fourteen hours traveling from Mexico to Michigan. It was bad enough she'd missed her connection, but then they'd lost her luggage. She waited an hour and gave up, asking them to send it home when they found it.

At least she had the important stuff: her Bible, book of inspirational quotes and digital card with the hundreds of pictures she'd taken on the mission trip. She couldn't wait to upload the shots to her Faithgirl blog.

"Ana-sta-sia," she called out. The cat was sure to be in attack mode. After all, Krista had abandoned her for nearly two weeks. How dare she!

"Kitty, kitty, kitty," Krista said, feeling her way down the hall to the kitchen.

It wasn't like Krista had completely abandoned her. Her best friend, Natalie Brown, stopped by to check on the feline.

The wall phone rang, making Krista yelp.

She snatched the receiver. "Hello?"

"Welcome home!" Natalie said.

"Thanks, I'm glad to be home. Just wish I had some light." She ran her hand across the wall in search of the switch.

"What do you mean?"

"The cat ate through my lamp cords." She flicked the switch but the ceiling light didn't come on. "Did I forget to pay my bill? No, I set it up on bill pay before I left."

"They wouldn't turn off your lights if you missed one payment, silly girl."

"I'm a tired girl and I can't see what I'm doing and any second now Anastasia is going to strike."

"But it was a good trip, right?" Natalie asked.

"It was amazing." Her heart filled with pride at the memory of helping the children in the small Mexican village. "Anything happen while I was gone?"

"Fred Skripps won the fishing contest, the new condo complex on Fourth got approved and they're bringing in a busload of tourists Friday. Be ready, tea mistress."

"Ready is my middle name."

"Bad, Krista, really bad."

"Sorry. Long flight, they lost my luggage and I'm hungry."

"Check your refrigerator."

Krista made her way to the fridge and pulled it open. Unfortunately the fridge light wasn't working either, but moonlight lit the kitchen enough for Krista to see her friend had left her some goodies.

"You're wonderful," Krista said.

"Says the woman who just spent ten days on a mission trip. You're welcome. There's chicken casserole, fresh fruit and takeout from Pekadill's."

"My mouth is watering. But if my power's out I can't heat it in the micro."

"Did you check the fuse box in the garage?" Nat offered.

"That's next. If I don't fall asleep on my way out there."

"Anastasia would have a field day with that."

"Did you see her at all?" Krista fumbled in the kitchen junk drawer.

"Once, the first time I stopped by. She thought I was you."

"How'd that go?" Krista pulled out a red mini flashlight.

"She ran, hid and never came out again."

"Except to trash my living room," Krista said.

"You want me to send Timothy over?"

"No, thanks. I'll be fine."

"He wouldn't mind."

"I'm good, really." Krista liked being able to take care of herself. Natalie had done plenty, and Krista didn't like taking advantage of Natalie's boyfriend's good nature. "I'll give you a call tomorrow."

"I'll stop by the tea shop."

"Sounds good."

She hung up and pointed the flashlight into the living room. "Kitty, kitty." She aimed in all the corners, above the bookshelf, then got down on her knees and held her breath as she flashed the light beneath the sofas.

"This is ridiculous." She stood. "I'm not going to let you punk me, kitty."

Pointing the flashlight ahead of her, she marched into the kitchen and flung open the back door. The smell of winter floated through the yard, wrapping around her shoulders like a soft blanket.

Home. There was nothing like it.

She marched outside to the detached garage. Shoving the flashlight into her sweater pocket, she heaved open the garage door and reached for her flashlight. A crashing sound made her jump back.

"Anastasia, how did you get in here?" Krista aimed the flashlight into the garage—

And screamed at the sight of a large man rummaging through her toolbox.

Instinct demanded she run, but for a second she couldn't move. Then the intruder turned to reveal a skeleton-masked face. He was holding a weapon in his hand.

Panic shot her out of the garage, her heart pounding against her chest. She raced for the house, focusing on the open door...

The man shoved her from behind and she went down against the cobblestone walk, the breath knocked from her lungs. It couldn't end like this. Who would run the tea shop?

Oh, of all the things to be worried about.

Eyes pinched shut, she braced herself.

But nothing happened.

She heard crunching of footsteps through the dormant garden as the man raced off. Could he be some homeless guy trying to stay warm?

"Hey!" a male voice called out behind her.

Followed by a pop. Then another.

She swallowed back the panic that threatened to make her sick.

Special Agent Luke McIntyre hit the ground when he saw the weapon aimed in his direction. Taking cover behind the house, he slipped his Glock from his belt and waited. He didn't want a shoot-out in this small town, but he had to defend himself.

And the woman.

Luke counted to three and poked his head out. The guy was out of sight.

A car's engine sputtered and cracked. Luke raced around the house in time to spot a dark green minivan peeling away from the curb. On the ground lay a nail gun.

Neighbors' lights popped on with interest and he quickly holstered his gun.

There was no doubt Krista Yates was in trouble.

Luke busted tail to get to Wentworth after the tip came in about Victor Garcia. The drug lord was sending men to the quiet Michigan town to finish some business with the Peace Church mission group. Garcia was a bold one to be using a church group to move drugs, but it didn't surprise Luke.

Garcia had been on the DEA's watch list for months and just when they thought they had enough to bring him in, the drug lord fled, probably to Mexico. Luke's office thought they'd lost him for good.

But Luke hadn't given up. Not on this one. There was too much history, too much at stake.

Luke slipped into town and touched base with the police chief, asking that Luke's position as DEA agent be confidential so as not to alert Garcia's men and chase them off. Luke knew that gossip in a small town traveled like wildfire.

Luke wanted to catch Garcia's men in the act of retrieving the drugs so he could hurt Victor Garcia where he'd feel it most: in his business.

No, Luke didn't just want to hurt Garcia. He wanted to destroy him.

The chief explained that Krista Yates coordinated the mission trip, and had somehow missed her connection, so she was arriving later than the rest of the group.

The question was, what was Garcia's connection to Krista Yates?

Luke started around back, the sound of sirens blaring in the distance. He pulled out his shield and clipped it to his jacket pocket. Didn't want Barney Fife thinking he was the perp.

He turned the corner.

The woman was gone.

"Miss Yates?" he called out.

"Who are you and what did you do with my cat?"

He turned toward the house. She was aiming a fire extinguisher at him.

He raised his hands and bit back a smile at her aggressive stance. "I'm a federal agent, ma'am." He nodded toward his shield.

"Oh." She put down the extinguisher. "Wait, how did you get here so fast? Did you say federal agent?"

He took a step toward her and stopped. She looked shaken, petrified. He couldn't blame her.

"Yes, ma'am. I'm with the DEA."

Her green eyes were innocent, yet weary, and a bruise was starting to form on her cheek.

"You'd better ice your cheek or you're gonna look like Rocky Balboa after ten rounds in the ring." Lowering his hands, he started for the house.

She reached for the fire extinguisher.

"I'm on your side, remember?" he said.

"Then fix my lights."

"Excuse me?"

"There's no light in my house. I went to the garage to check the fuse box and that guy jumped me, I mean jumped over me." She shook her head in confusion.

"Go on inside and I'll check the fuse box."

"It's dark inside."

"Okay, then wait on the porch. The cops should be pulling up any second now."

She hugged her midsection with one hand and clutched a charm at the base of her neck with the other. Although she acted strong, she looked broken and terrified.

And way too fragile.

Luke went into the garage, pulled out his pen flashlight and inspected the fuse box. As he expected, all switches were in the Off position. Luke snapped them on and light beamed from the house onto the back porch.

"Want me to close the garage door?" he called.

No answer.

Luke peered out from the garage. The woman was gone. What the heck? Did the guy come back? Send an accomplice? He started for the house.

"Police! Freeze!" a female shouted from behind him.

Luke raised his hands. "I'm a federal officer."

"Yeah and I'm Judge Judy. Get down on the ground."

"If you'd let me turn around—"

"Do it!" The woman sounded too young and green to be holding a firearm.

The guys in Luke's division would have a field day if the pipsqueak cop shot him in the back due to lack of experience.

"I'm going, I'm going." Luke dropped to his knees, interlacing his hands behind his head.

"All the way down!"

He hesitated, bitter memories tearing through his chest. Being forced down...

Held there while his partner, Karl, fought for his life.

"I said get down!" she ordered.

"Deanna, what are you doing?" the Yates woman said, coming out of the house.

"Stay in the house, Krista," the cop ordered.

"No, he's a good guy."

Good? Hardly.

Krista walked up to Luke, removed his shield and flashed it at the cop.

He doubted the rookie could see past her adrenaline rush.

Luke heard another car pull up.

"How do you know that's real?" the female cop said.

"It's real," a man offered.

Luke recognized Chief Cunningham's voice. Luke had spent a good hour with him earlier tonight going over the case.

"Lower your weapon, Officer West," the chief said.

From the concerned look on Krista's face, Luke sensed the female cop didn't follow the order. This was probably the most action she'd seen in her entire year on the force. If she'd even been on the force a year.

"West!" the chief threatened.

Krista sighed with relief and touched Luke's shoulder. "You need help getting up?"

Right, he still hadn't moved, paralyzed by the dark memories that he couldn't bury deep enough. Guilt had a way of rising to the surface to mess with your head at the worst possible moments.

Krista gripped his arm to help him stand. As if he needed help from this fragile thing.

Fragile. Innocent. Dangerous.

"I'm fine." Luke stood and turned to the cop. She looked barely twenty.

"Sorry about that," the chief offered.

"No problem," Luke said.

"Yes problem," Krista countered.

They all looked at her.

"Anastasia is missing." With a shake of her head, she went into the house.

Luke glanced at the chief. "Who's Anastasia?"

"Her cat," Officer West said.

Luke glanced at the house. Krista had nearly been taken out by a member of Garcia's gang and all she could think about was a silly cat?

"Officer West, continue your patrol and don't tell anyone about Agent McIntyre's presence in town," Chief Cunningham said. "I'll handle things here."

"The guy who jumped Miss Yates was driving a dark green minivan," Luke said.

"Okay, thanks." Officer West walked to her cruiser.

"These are not teenage pranksters, West. Radio in if you spot the van. That's an order," the chief said.

"Yes, sir."

The chief turned to Luke. "Ready?"

"For what?"

The chief started for the house. "I have a feeling Krista isn't going to be in a talking mood until we find her cat."

"You're kidding."

"Welcome to Wentworth, son." Chief Cunningham climbed the steps and disappeared into the house.

"Fantastic," Luke muttered.

He was allergic to cats, and even more allergic to small towns. He grew up in one and hightailed it out of there before he hit his seventeenth birthday. There was too much gossip in a small town, too much imagined drama.

He climbed the steps and glanced across the yard. Imagined? Most of the time. In Krista Yates's case he was pretty sure she'd brought it home with her from Mexico, probably in her luggage, or in something she saw or said.

He shook his head. She was a talker, for sure, but he couldn't imagine the sweet-faced blonde saying anything offensive or rude. This wasn't about manners, it was about one of Mexico's biggest drug cartels moving product into the country via innocents.

The Yates woman defined innocent.

Luke stepped into the house and found the chief and Krista in the living room. "So the house was like this when you got home?" the chief said, eyeing the mess.

"I thought it was the cat."

"You thought the cat tipped over your end table?" Luke asked.

"She's a really big cat and she's rather upset with me right now."

"The sooner we can get a description of the man you saw in the garage, the more accurate it will be," the chief said.

"You don't think he killed her, do you?" Krista asked, her eyes rounding with fear. Wide, green, helpless eyes.

"Now, why would he kill your cat, Krista?" the chief said.

Krista narrowed her eyes. "You, of all people, should not be asking me that. Gladys still has scars from the quilting open house."

"Point taken."

"Anastasia? Here, kitty, kitty." She glanced at Luke. "Get the Whiskas. On top of the microwave." She disappeared upstairs.

Luke glanced at the chief.

"The sooner we find the cat…" the chief said with a shrug.

Luke found the bag of cat treats in the kitchen. As he grabbed them, his gaze caught on a photograph on the windowsill of a teenage Krista, and he guessed her mom, and perhaps grandmother. They looked like a team, arms around each other, ready to take on the world.

They were a loving family. He'd always wondered what that looked like.

It's not like he hung out with the guys at work and their families. He'd had a few invitations, but he knew he didn't belong and would make everyone feel awkward.

He never seemed to belong.

And that was fine by him.

"I got the cat treats!" he called out, more than a bit irritated with this diversion from their course of finding her attacker.

The chief was on the phone, and Luke started up the stairs. Krista met him halfway.

"No shouting," she whispered.

"I was shouting?"

"You shake and I'll grab."

"Excuse me?"

"The cat. You go ahead of me and shake the bag and I'll grab her when she comes out."

"Ma'am, we really need to talk about—"

"Shake and grab."

If the guys found out about this, he'd be more of a laughing stock than if he'd been shot by Rookie West.

She motioned for him to slip around her. The staircase was narrow and he couldn't help but brush up against her as he passed. She smelled fresh, like flowers, even after a twelve-plus-hour flight. How was that possible?

Shaking the bag, he started down the hallway, glancing into a bedroom. Neat and tidy, the four-poster bed was covered with a down comforter and the curtains looked handmade.

"Kitty, kitty. I love you, kitty," she crooned.

He kept shaking, ignoring the generous use of a word he'd rarely heard growing up. What the heck was wrong with him tonight?

Lack of sleep. He'd gone too long on five hours a night. It was bound to catch up to him.

"Wait." She touched his arm.

Warmth seeped through his leather jacket as he eyed her petite fingers.

She pointed to the next bedroom and released him,

tiptoeing ahead. He glanced at his arm, struggling to remember the last time he'd felt any gentle, nonthreatening human contact.

Yeah, man, you do need sleep.

After he nailed Garcia and his production line. After the murderer was in jail. After…

What? There'd always be another Garcia.

Luke's job would never be over and he'd never be satisfied.

Krista crooked her finger and he followed her into the bedroom. This one had to be hers. A canopy bed centered the room, draped in light purple and pink material. A Bible lay on her nightstand and a tray of antique perfume bottles lined her dresser.

Luke glanced away.

Krista pressed her fingers to her lips and kneeled down pointing beneath the bed. He motioned to the bag of treats and she nodded for him to shake. He shook. They waited. No cat.

"Oh, boy. She's gotta be under here." Krista shimmied beneath the bed.

He felt something brush against his pants and glanced down to see a black-and-white cat doing a figure eight around his legs.

"Miss Yates?" he said.

"Yeah?" her muffled voice answered.

"Is this the cat you're looking for?"

She wiggled back out and sat cross-legged on the floor. "Anastasia?" With a confused frown she glanced up at Luke. "She hates people."

"I'm not people. I'm a federal officer, remember?" He smiled, hoping she'd be able to shift gears quickly and give them the intruder's description before too many other things clouded her memory.

"Wow." She looked up at him with awe. Respect.

He didn't deserve it.

"Not a big deal." He passed her the treat bag and she opened it.

The cat pounced on Krista. "Okay, okay," she laughed, a sweet, carefree sound.

"About your statement…" he said.

The cat purred and rubbed against Krista's knee as she put a treat on the hardwood floor.

"Ready?" he said.

"Sure." She stood and Luke automatically reached out to steady her. He withdrew his hand, afraid his touch might damage her somehow.

He turned to leave the room.

"Wait a second, can you hold this?" She handed him the treat bag.

She put her hands together and stood at her dresser. "Thank you, Lord, for allowing me to help such wonderful children in Mexico, for seeing me home safely, for my friends, for Anastasia and for Agent Luke for being my hero tonight. Amen."

He wanted to correct her, tell her he was no one's hero, not by any stretch of the imagination.

"Okay, let's get this over with," she said. "I'm exhausted."

She took a step toward the door, wearing that pleasant smile.

The crack of a gunshot echoed through the window. Luke grabbed her and hit the floor.

TWO

Here she was, knocked on the ground again. Not exactly how she pictured her first night home. She'd hoped to get into a bubble bath to wash the plane scum from her skin, sip a cup of chamomile tea and crawl beneath her down comforter.

Instead, someone was shooting at her.

"Stay here." Agent McIntyre stood and pressed his back against the wall.

"But the cat—"

He pressed two fingers to his lips to shush her. His expression was fierce, intense. She was glad she wasn't on his bad side. She started to get up.

"Right there," he ordered, slipping a gun from inside his jacket.

Her breath caught at the memory of little Armando Morales. Images of the little boy covered in blood, moaning in pain, made her freeze in place. Armando had been an innocent bystander caught in a territorial shoot-out among drug dealers.

Yet he was just a child.

The whole experience reminded her how lucky she

was. She may not have had a father or siblings, but she lived a safe, healthy life in Wentworth.

At least she had…until tonight.

The stairs creaked as Agent McIntyre went to investigate. She scooted to the door and leaned into the doorjamb, wishing that this was some kind of crazy dream brought on by exhaustion. Sure, she'd returned home, downed a few scoops of casserole and had crawled into bed. The peas in the casserole didn't agree with her, sparking nightmares that began with her being chased down by her garage stalker.

Another popping sound shattered that wishful thinking. It sounded farther away than the first, definitely from outside. Her windows hadn't been shattered by the shots.

"Anastasia?" she whispered, needing a hug, even from a crazy cat.

Hugs were something she sorely missed since Gran passed away and Mom moved to Florida with Lenny. Krista missed a lot of things and had hoped to fill that emptiness with her missionary work with kids, and maybe, in the not too distant future, a loving husband and children of her own.

Only, she was a disaster in the relationship department and had decided to stop looking so hard. She prayed about her life, asked God to help her find inner peace.

Kind of hard to find peace when people are shooting at you.

"Miss Yates?" Agent McIntyre called from the bottom of the stairs.

"Yes?"

"It's safe. You can come down."

She headed downstairs where the intense, yet handsome, agent was waiting for her. Her eyes caught on the gun in his hand and she froze.

He glanced at his weapon. "Sorry." He shoved it into its holster and pulled his jacket over it to conceal the weapon.

"The gunshot?" she asked.

"A neighbor was trying to scare off a raccoon. The chief's out there talking to him now."

"Probably the Bender kid. Someone should tell his dad to lock up the rifle."

"I'll be sure to do that. Come on, let's take your statement about the man in the garage before you fall asleep on us."

She ambled through the living room. "With all this adrenaline rushing through my body I doubt I'll ever sleep again."

Anastasia raced past her into the kitchen.

"How about some tea?" she offered over her shoulder.

"I'm good, thanks."

Was he ever. Agent McIntyre was good at being there to protect Krista, acting confident and unshakable. He was pretty nice to look at, too.

Warning! Sleep alert!

She was not one to ogle a stranger, but she was tired,

hungry and confused. A man had broken into her house and garage. Looking for what? And wait a second, why was a federal agent at her house?

She turned to him. "Hey, you never told me why you're here."

"First things first. Let's get ice for your cheek."

She touched her face. "It looks bad?"

"Not yet, but it will if you don't ice it." He took a kitchen towel from the rack, opened the freezer and dropped a handful of cubes in it. He reached out to place it on the bruise and she took it from him.

"Thanks," she said, holding it in place and leaning against the counter. "You're an expert at first aid?"

"I've been knocked down a few times."

Yeah, she could see that. He was tough, the kind of man who stayed focused and didn't back down from a fight.

"Ready to give a statement?" he said.

"Sure."

Chief Cunningham stepped into the kitchen from the back door. "I gave the Bender kid a lecture about firearms. Took away the rifle for the time being, until his dad gets back from his business trip."

"I was about to question Miss Yates," Agent McIntyre said.

"Please call me Krista. Miss Yates makes me feel like an old maid."

"Okay, Krista." Agent McIntyre sat at the kitchen table and opened a small notebook.

Good, he looked less intimidating sitting instead

of towering over her. The man had to be over six feet tall, dwarfing her five-foot-three-inch frame. His good looks and hard-edged demeanor made her uncomfortable. He was different than the few men she'd dated in Wentworth.

Not just different. He was a cynical man who'd chosen a violent career.

She sighed and found a bag of chamomile tea. She'd lost her dad to violence and saw what violence did to innocent children on her mission trips. Krista believed in discussing problems, praying about them. She wondered if a man like Luke McIntyre ever prayed. She doubted it.

"Can you describe the man in your garage?"

"No, I'm sorry. He was wearing a skeleton mask."

The agent hesitated in his note taking. Why?

"Did anything unusual happen at the airport in Mexico before you boarded?" he continued, focusing his blue-green eyes on his notepad. She'd noticed their brilliant color when he'd helped her trap Anastasia.

"Nothing unusual other than missing my first flight, which meant missing my connection in Chicago, and then losing my luggage."

"Did anyone talk to you at the airport?"

"Not really."

"Anyone at all. The slightest, seemingly insignificant conversation could help us."

"I chatted with a young mother. She had the cutest little newborn."

"Any men?"

"I don't like talking to men."

The agent snapped his eyes to meet hers. "You don't talk to men?"

"Strangers. I don't trust them."

"Smart girl."

Irked, she turned her back to him and poured hot water into the cup. "Thank you, Agent McIntyre, but I stopped being a girl ten years ago."

Silence filled the room. She'd overreacted. She couldn't help it. Being called a "girl" hit a nerve.

It reminded her of when she was a little girl, innocent and trusting. When she made the mistake of talking to a stranger.

"Anyway, no talking with strangers," she said, turning to Agent McIntyre.

Chief Cunningham stood quietly in the corner, arms crossed over his chest. He knew the story, the loss and devastation to the Yates family. The chief was the only one who knew the truth, knew that Mom and Krista had fled to Wentworth from California because the little girl had been so close to a killer, looked him in the eye, even shook his hand.

Krista had been only five when she'd told the stranger that Father was still at work in the Lincoln building. No one could have anticipated how that bit of information would change everyone's lives. It led the disheartened investor to Dad's office where an argument turned violent and Dad was killed.

After Dad's death, Mom fretted that the killer would come back for Krista since she'd seen him, so Mom packed up their belongings and moved to Gran's house in Michigan. A year later they got word that Dad's killer had been caught and sentenced to life in prison.

Krista was safe, but Mom and Gran couldn't drop the overprotective parenting style. Mom probably would have objected to Krista going on the mission trip if she'd still been living in Wentworth.

"And when you landed in Grand Rapids?" the agent asked, interrupting her thoughts.

"I got paged."

"For what?"

"Someone found my license, but I had my license so it was a mix-up. By the time I got to baggage claim, I discovered they'd lost my luggage."

"Did you get there as luggage was coming out on the conveyor belt?"

"No."

"So someone could have taken your luggage?"

"I guess, by accident, sure."

The agent and police chief exchanged glances.

"I don't have anything worth stealing, if that's where you're going with this."

"You might have had something you didn't know you had," Agent McIntyre said.

Then again his job was to see conspiracy around every corner.

"Why are you here again?" she asked and sipped her tea with one hand, while holding the ice to her cheek with the other.

"I'm investigating drug trafficking from Mexico into the Midwest."

"You think they used my suitcase to smuggle drugs?" she said, her voice pitched with disbelief.

"It's not that simple," Agent McIntyre said.

"What, then?"

"We got a tip that the leader of the drug cartel sent men to Michigan to tie up some loose ends with a church group. The tip came shortly after your group left Mexicali."

"So, you think someone in the mission group was smuggling drugs?"

"It's a possibility, yes," McIntyre said.

"No. It's not. I know you're used to dealing with criminals, Agent McIntyre, but people like us don't break the law."

"Luke."

"Excuse me?"

"My name is Luke. You don't have to call me Agent McIntyre."

"Oh, okay." But it wasn't okay. She didn't want to call him by his first name, didn't like the fact he was accusing someone in her church of smuggling and she didn't like that he was still here at nearly one in the morning.

"Is that all?" she said.

"You didn't recognize anything about the assailant?"

"The man in the garage? No. He could have been some teenager fooling around for all I know."

"Krista, I want you to stay with me and Jane tonight," Chief Cunningham said.

"Thank you, chief, but I'm fine here."

"You're really not," Luke interjected.

"You don't know that for sure."

"Why risk it?" he said.

"What about staying with your friend, Natalie, or the Sass family?" the chief suggested.

"Look, I haven't had a good night's sleep in nearly two weeks. I need to sleep in my own bed!" she shouted, then slapped her hand to her mouth. She didn't mean to lose it like that. "Sorry, I get cranky when I'm tired."

"I'll stay with her," Luke said to the chief.

"No, really, that's okay." She wasn't sure what scared her more: the stranger jumping out of her garage or the handsome agent offering to sleep under the same roof.

"Krista, you either stay at our house or with the Sasses, or let Agent McIntyre bunk on your couch. You pick."

No one had spent the night since Mom came back for Gran's funeral two years ago. Mom had moved to Florida with Lenny, and since Gran's death Krista had been in the family house alone.

And tonight they were asking her to share it with a stranger.

"I won't let a strange man stay in my house," she said.

"I'm a federal agent and I'm here to protect you. What's the problem?"

"It doesn't look right," she said.

Agent McIntyre glanced at the chief.

"Small town, people talk," the chief explained. He glanced at Krista. "We'll tell them Agent McIntyre is my nephew from upstate New York."

"I don't like lying," Krista said.

"Undercover work isn't the same as lying," Luke said. "It'll help me figure out who's behind all this."

"I understand, but—"

"How about I stay in the loft above your garage? I noticed a room up there."

"Great idea," Chief Cunningham offered. "It's well insulated and heated since the previous owner ran his mechanics business out of the garage."

"It's pretty gross up there," Krista said, feeling bad that she couldn't offer better accommodations.

"I'm sure I've slept in worse."

She wondered what could be worse than a cold, damp garage.

"It's a good compromise," the chief offered. "He can keep an eye on the house from the garage."

True, he could see her bedroom window from the garage. A thought that was both comforting and unsettling.

"It's either your garage or my car," Luke said. "And I don't want your neighbors to think I'm stalking you from the street."

"Okay, fine. There's a cot up there, although we haven't used it in years."

"I wasn't planning on sleeping much anyway."

Of course not. He'd be watching the house. Watching her.

"I'll have patrol swing by every hour." The chief shook Agent McIntyre's hand. "You'll check in tomorrow?"

"Yes, sir."

"Good night, Krista."

"Good night. Thanks, chief."

The chief walked out to his cruiser and Luke hesitated at the back door.

"You should have better security. Anyone could pop one of these windows and—"

"This is not New York City," she argued.

"You're right about that." He turned to her, scribbling something in his notebook.

Probably that she was a smarty-pants, disagreeable, cat-obsessed, crazy woman.

"You ever consider getting a dog?" he said.

"Not really, why?"

"They make great alarm systems."

"You're a dog person?"

"That surprises you?" He looked at her.

It did actually. Dog people were loving and kind. This man seemed guarded and cynical.

"Kind of, I mean, Anastasia adores you and she usually hates dog people."

"Told you that, did she?"

Was he joking with her? No, she was just exhausted and imagining it.

He glanced out the window and back at Krista. "Good night, then."

"Wait, I'll get you some blankets and a pillow." She went upstairs to the hall closet and pulled out pink linens. She guessed not his usual color, but pale pinks and purples were her favorite and she'd decorated the house accordingly.

She wasn't used to having company and wondered what else he needed.

He's not company. He's a cop after a criminal.

What did the man look like? What color was his hair? His eyes? What did he say?

Childhood memories assaulted her. She'd tried to describe the man who came looking for her dad, but she was too upset that Daddy wasn't coming home. Ever.

She hugged the linens and made for the stairs. She thought she'd put it behind her, buried the memories and the fear so deep that they wouldn't rise to scare the wits out of her.

But danger was back, in the form of the DEA agent bunking in her garage.

How on earth did she get embroiled in this mystery? She refused to believe someone on the mission trip had a connection to a drug organization. She just wouldn't accept it.

"Here," she said, stepping into the kitchen.

Agent McIntyre was eyeing photos lined up on the window ledge.

"Your mom and…?" he asked.

"Grandmother. We moved here when—" She stopped short. She couldn't even talk about it. "We moved here when I was five."

He turned and eyed her with speculation. She shoved the linens at him. "This should keep you warm. Sorry about the color."

He took the blankets and pillow. "Hopefully I won't break out in hives."

He was teasing again? She wasn't sure, couldn't be sure of anything right now.

"Yes, well." She opened the back door. "I'm up and out by eight to prep the tea shop for customers."

He stepped onto the back porch and turned to her. "I'm right outside if you need me."

He shot her a half smile, his blue eyes sparkling with color. Oh, heavens, she was tired all right.

"Thanks, good night," she said.

"Lock up behind me."

She shut the door and clicked the lock. He nodded his approval through the window and headed out to the garage.

He's just doing his job, Krista.

Sure, intellectually she knew that, but emotionally? Emotionally she heard Gran's and Mom's worried voices, felt the iron hand of control clamp down on her shoulders. They'd meant it out of love, but sometimes she just couldn't breathe.

Where are you going, Krista? What did you do today? Who did you talk to?

It wasn't until she was in her late teens did they explain that the protective habit was born out of love. They loved her so much they didn't want to see her hurt by a stranger. They'd developed the habit because years ago they'd feared for her safety after her father was killed.

Agent McIntyre wasn't motivated by love, but rather by duty. He'd stay over Krista's garage and unravel this threat before anyone got hurt. She sensed he was a warrior type, a controlling force.

Krista turned off the kitchen light and headed upstairs. She didn't want a controlling force in her life. She'd fought long and hard for her independence. She'd practically begged Mom to relocate to Florida with Lenny. Krista didn't want Mom missing out on wonderful years of retirement with her new husband because she had some irrational fear about Krista being hurt.

The past was the past, long gone, buried with the news that Dad's killer had died in prison.

It had been years since the nightmare resurfaced to haunt Krista. Yet tonight, thanks to a stranger breaking into her house and the DEA agent sleeping in her garage, the violence was back in her life.

Along with the memories.

THREE

The Yates woman might have been exhausted last night, but she woke up with more energy than a kid on a gummy bear high.

By eight she was out the door, headed to the family tea shop. Luke followed close behind, both to protect her and to look for insight into this woman, her friends and the townspeople. Insight that would give him a clue as to who might be Victor Garcia's drug mule. The criminal wouldn't be stupid enough to actually smuggle drugs through Krista's luggage, would he? No, Luke sensed something else was going on. He just didn't know what.

He'd tried talking Krista out of opening the shop today, suggesting she needed a day to recover from her trip. But she was having none of it. She told him this time of year, right before the holidays, people needed the respite from their busy lives to enjoy a cup a tea. She'd said, "It's not about the tea. It's about friendship and connections."

Two things completely foreign to Luke.

Sitting in the back of Grace's Tea Shop, he read the

paper to get a handle on the local flavor. He glanced around the shop, painted in pale purple with frilly lace framing the windows. Dainty chairs bordered small, round tables and a lit fireplace took the chill out of the morning air.

Luke did not belong here. This was a woman's place, a peaceful place.

"Coffee?" Krista offered, walking up to him with a pot. She looked enchanting this morning with her long, blond hair pulled back and her cheeks rosy from cooking scones and muffins.

"I thought you specialized in tea?" he said.

"I figured you were a coffee kind of guy."

"You figured right."

He wondered what else she'd figured out about him.

She poured him a cup and said, "Black, right?"

He nodded. "I think we should come up with a story about why I'm here at the tea shop."

"You're a customer, simple enough."

"I have a feeling I'm not your usual demographic."

"I've had men in here before."

He raised an eyebrow. "Really?"

"Okay, well, not every day, but occasionally."

"To ease suspicion, we'll go with the story that I'm Chief Cunningham's nephew and you hired me as your temporary handyman."

She rested the coffeepot on the table. "I told you, I'm not into lying, especially to my friends."

"Then I'll be the chief's friend, and you can give me

a list of things you need fixed. I'll be your handyman for real."

She narrowed her eyes.

"What? I'm pretty good with a hammer." Working on his own house had been cathartic after Karl's death.

She placed the coffeepot on the warmer and pulled vegetables from the refrigerator. "I'll think about it."

He could tell the thought of Luke shadowing her, being close, made her uncomfortable. He wasn't sure if it was because he was a constant reminder of the threat hiding in the shadows, or if it was something else.

Maybe she sensed the darkness that haunted him and knew instinctively to keep her distance. From him.

He sipped his coffee and remarked how good it tasted. "What's in this?"

"A secret ingredient." She winked.

He snapped his attention back to the paper. She was too nice, too gentle and it made him uncomfortable.

A tall brunette breezed into the back, oblivious to Luke's presence. The woman was dressed in a tailored suit and high heels. Her perfume filled the kitchen, the smell a sharp contrast to Krista's subtle floral scent.

"She's back!" The brunette rushed to Krista and gave her a hug. "How'd you sleep?"

"Pretty good." Krista motioned to Luke. "This is Luke. Luke, this is Natalie."

The woman turned to Luke, her eyes flaring with interest.

Luke stood and extended his hand. "I'm a friend of Chief Cunningham."

"Well, hello."

They shook hands.

"How long are you staying in Wentworth?" Natalie asked.

"Not sure. A few weeks, I guess."

"Wonderful." She winked at Krista.

Krista blushed. "Knock it off."

Could Krista really be that shy and innocent? One more reason Luke should stay close. She'd be an easy target for one of Garcia's men. Because she coordinated the mission trip, Luke had to assume Garcia's men would come looking for her first when they got to town. That is, if they weren't already here.

Yet if last night's intruder was with the Garcia operation, he would have done more to Krista than hurdle her and flee the scene.

A short guy, late thirties, marched into the back of the shop. Busy place, and they weren't even open for business yet.

"Krista!" the man said, wrapping his arms around her for a hug. He was either oblivious to Luke or was purposely ignoring him.

Krista made a face at her girlfriend over the man's shoulder and broke the hug. "Good to see you, Alan. I've got to check the soups." She went to stir a pot on the stove.

"I heard the Bender kid shot out your windows last night," Alan said.

"No, they didn't shoot out her windows," Natalie

offered. "A stranger was caught rifling through her garage."

"Right on both counts," Krista said.

"Alan, meet the chief's friend," Natalie said, introducing them.

The man turned and his jaw hardened. Alan was in his mid-thirties, clean-shaven with perfectly combed hair and suspicious eyes. He was about four inches shorter than Luke's six-foot-one-inch frame.

Luke shook hands with Alan, who squeezed extra tight. He was making his mark, letting Luke know Krista was off-limits. Whatever. Luke wasn't here for romance and he surely wouldn't get involved with a fragile creature like Krista Yates.

"Nice to meet you, Alan," Luke said.

Alan nodded and turned back to Krista. "So, what really happened last night?"

"Someone broke into the house and the garage," she said.

"What?" Natalie said. "I was there at six to check on Anastasia. Oh, my goodness, is she okay?"

"She's fine. I'm fine. Everything's fine." Krista waved them off and went back to stirring the soup.

"Krista, are you really okay?" Alan placed his hand on her shoulder.

Krista stopped stirring for a second, then continued. Luke didn't miss the hesitation. Alan ignored it.

"I was a little rattled, but I'm okay," Krista said. "The cops got there right away."

"You shouldn't be living in that house alone," Alan said.

"Thanks, but I'm a big girl, Alan."

"She's not alone. I'm staying over the garage," Luke offered.

Alan and Natalie looked at Luke as if he'd just announced Martians had landed in the town square.

"My friend, the chief, was worried about the perpetrator coming back so he asked me to stay close," he explained.

"The perpetrator?" Alan said. "Are you a cop, too?"

"I've had some experience in law enforcement, yes."

"What kind of experience?" Alan pushed.

"You want my résumé?" Luke pushed back.

"Take the discussion outside, guys," Krista said. "I've got to get moving if I'm going to open by eleven." She corralled everyone out the back.

Alan hesitated and turned to her. "Dinner tonight?"

"No, but thank you. I'm still jet-lagged."

Alan touched her arm. "You shouldn't have opened today, Krista."

"It's the busy season, you know that. The Christmas teas cover half my expenses for the year. I can't lose that revenue."

"But—"

"Look," she interrupted Alan. "I appreciate your concern, I really do. But the Sass twins won't clock in for another hour and I need to get back to work."

Natalie and Krista hugged. Krista stepped back into the shop before Alan could get another hug. She shut the door, leaving the three of them standing by the herb garden.

Luke's cell vibrated and he checked the caller ID. It was his supervisor, Agent Marks.

"Excuse me," he said to Alan and Natalie.

With a nod, Luke walked to his car and answered his cell.

"McIntyre," he said.

"Any progress?" Agent Marks questioned.

"Not yet, sir."

"Did Miss Yates recognize last night's assailant?"

"He was wearing a mask."

"Do you want to bring her in for protection?"

"She'd fight me on it." Luke saw in her eyes how devoted she was to her business and it sounded like this was the prime season for revenues.

"It's your call. I've put an alert out on her luggage."

"Thanks."

"Be careful," Marks warned. "And call for backup if you need it."

"Yes, sir."

He pocketed his phone and eyed the tea shop, an old brick house converted into a small restaurant in the heart of town.

"Nice meeting you," Natalie called out to Luke as she breezed to her older-model Volvo in the parking lot.

"You, too," he said.

With a curt nod, Alan walked to a newer SUV and

took off. Luke noted Alan's license plate and would call it in later. There was something about that guy...

Luke couldn't be jealous, not over a complete stranger like Krista. More like, his protective instincts were kicking in. He'd seen how Krista needed space, didn't like Alan touching her. Whatever that guy thought of their relationship, Krista had a completely different take on things.

Luke should head back to Krista's house, get tools and start his handyman cover. Instinct told him not to leave her alone, not even for a few minutes. He called the chief's private line.

"Cunningham," the chief answered.

"It's Luke McIntyre."

"Everything okay?"

"Yes, sir. I was wondering if you could do me a favor and swing by the tea shop with some tools. I'd rather not leave Krista alone."

"Put you to work, did she?"

"Not officially, but I'm trying to convince her it's a good cover."

He chuckled. "I'll bring by my toolbox. We think we got something on the perp's car. A dark green minivan with an Ohio plate was dumped on the other side of Silver Lake. Fits the description."

"So the guy's still close."

"Looks that way."

A scream echoed from the tea shop and Luke bolted for the house.

FOUR

He should have checked the entire building, every corner, beneath every table, inside every teapot before leaving her alone in there.

He whipped the back door open. "Krista!"

Nothing.

"No, no," he ground out between clenched teeth. He raced to the stairs leading to the second-floor office. Taking the stairs two at a time, he pulled out his firearm, got to the top and spun around, pointing the gun into the room.

Directly at Krista.

With round, terrified green eyes, she dropped the teapot in her hands and it crashed to the floor into pieces. He swung the gun around the room.

They were alone.

"What happened?" He holstered his gun. He took a step toward her and she backed up.

She was scared out of her mind. Because of Luke.

He put out his hands in a calming gesture. "I'm sorry about the gun. Okay? Just breathe."

Luke took a deep breath and she mimicked him.

"Are you okay?" he asked.

She nodded affirmative.

"You screamed. Why?" He didn't move, didn't step closer. But he wanted to. He wanted to put his arm around her and calm her down, stop her trembling.

His touch would probably make her shake more considering he'd just pulled a gun on her.

"What happened?" he asked.

She pointed to the broken teapot on the floor. Lying beside it was a dead mouse.

"That's why you screamed?"

She nodded again. "It was…in the teapot. So, so I was checking other ones and you…" her voice hitched.

He threatened her with a gun.

"I'm sorry. I thought…never mind. I tend to go to the worst-case-scenario places. But you're okay, that's all that matters. Everything's fine."

But it wasn't fine. There was no way a mouse could open the lid of a teapot and climb inside.

"Has this happened before?" he asked.

"We have mice problems. All restaurants do," she said, defensively.

Good, she was coming out of her fright.

"The teapot was on my desk when I came upstairs. Strange, because I don't remember leaving it here."

She touched the calendar desk pad. Somewhere, deep down, she sensed the danger as well. But for now, Luke would shelve the possibility of this being a threat against her and help her get her bearings back.

"Krista!" a girl called from downstairs.

Krista didn't answer at first. She just stared at Luke. He stepped aside, giving her ample room to pass. The last thing he wanted was to make her feel threatened. She needed to trust him if he had any chance of protecting her.

"I'll clean up," he said. "Broom?"

She pointed to the far end of the long attic office. He stepped around her and she rushed downstairs.

The high pitch of excited female voices drifted up from the restaurant. He grabbed the broom and hesitated, trying to calm the adrenaline rush. Couldn't help reacting the way he did. He'd been a few seconds too late and his partner died because of it. Luke wouldn't make that mistake again, especially not with a complete innocent like Krista.

With a deep breath, Luke got the broom and began sweeping up the mess. Shards of china, loose tea and a few candy wrappers.

He eyed the dead mouse. A few inches away he spotted a white scrap of paper folded a few times. He grabbed a pair of latex gloves used by the kitchen staff and opened the note.

Welcome Home, Pretty Lady.

"Great," Luke muttered. He had to assume this was a threat, right? A dead mouse in a teapot. So Garcia's man had been here in the shop?

"That's too close." It's not like the quaint tea shop would have video surveillance. He'd have to do it the old-fashioned way and check the locks for signs of tampering.

He took his time cleaning up, giving Krista space. She needed to recover from the sight of the dead mouse, and a man pointing a gun at her. But he wasn't going far. When the chief stopped by Luke would hand off the note and have him send it in for prints.

It seemed tame for a drug lord's henchman. Subtlety wasn't their style. They were more direct, more in-your-face vicious.

Now you get to watch him die.

Garcia's words slashed through Luke's chest like a knife. His best friend, the only guy in the world who both understood and accepted Luke for who he was, broken parts and all, died right in front of Luke. And he was unable to do a thing about it.

Luke shoved back the memory and the pain. Stuffing the note into a plastic baggie and then into his pocket, he headed downstairs to call in this development.

If only he knew what it meant.

Thank goodness Krista was feeling more like herself halfway through the lunch rush. She thought her nerves would never stop skittering.

First a break-in, then a dead mouse, then Luke aiming a gun directly at her chest.

She reminded herself that that was normal behavior for a man like Luke, but still, the image was not easy to shake. Pulling a gun because she'd found a dead mouse was definitely overkill. Then again, he didn't know what had made her scream.

"Table four needs more cream and jam," Tori Sass

said, breezing into the kitchen with a handful of plates.

"Right up." Krista squirted sweetened whipped cream onto a plate and spooned a dollop of jam beside it. Some liked their scones extra sweet. She wondered how Agent McIntyre liked his.

No, he'd probably never tried a scone. He seemed more the doughnut type of guy.

Why was she thinking about him again? She was tired, that's all. Tired and frightened out of her right mind between the mouse and firearm.

She'd never forget the look on his face when he'd swung around and pointed it at her. He looked powerful and determined.

And maybe a little frightened. Was that possible?

Sure, even in his line of work a person felt fear, she reminded herself.

"How's the order for table seven?" Tatum Sass asked.

"Almost there." Krista refocused on the tea sandwiches in front of her and arranged red rose petals in between them.

Make them feel special, Mom had taught her. It was Krista's role to give local women a place to gather, share dreams, hopes and fears, in a safe environment.

Yet Krista wasn't feeling safe right now. Between the jet lag, lack of sleep and this morning's excitement, she was exhausted and more than a little off kilter.

"You look tired," Tatum said, waiting for her order.

"Thanks, now I feel so much better," Krista joked.

"Why don't you take a break? This is the last food order."

Krista nodded. "I'll be out back."

She untied her apron and flung it over the hook. She could use a few minutes of fresh air. Luckily, it was unseasonably warm for a November day in Michigan, so she grabbed a sweater and stepped outside.

And spotted Luke trimming back the rose bushes. She'd meant to do that before her trip, before the fall hit. But she'd run out of time, what with the Sass girls starting up community college and having limited availability.

As Luke tended to the rose bush, she remarked how normal he looked, like a regular guy. Not like a violent man who packed a gun against his ribcage.

With seemingly gentle fingers, Luke snipped the rose stem with some kind of knife. A pocket knife.

"Hey, I've got pruning shears," she said.

He turned to her and she could have sworn she read regret in his eyes, probably because he'd scared the wits out of her earlier.

"Hang on," she said. She went back inside, dug into the white china cabinet and found the shears. As she opened the door to go back out, she nearly ran into him.

She didn't expect him to be so close. Nor did she expect her heart to skip a few beats. And not out of fear.

She handed him the shears. "Thanks."

"It's the least I can do considering I scared the—" he paused "—you know."

"Have you been out there all afternoon?"

"Pretty much."

"Did you get lunch?"

"Not yet."

"I'll make you a sandwich." She motioned him into the shop, but he hesitated.

"Come on, it's safe," she joked.

He followed her inside and washed his hands.

"Turkey okay?" she asked, putting on gloves.

"You even guessed my favorite sandwich? How do you do that?" He settled at a table in the back.

"Everyone likes turkey." She pulled out bread, lettuce and tomatoes.

Tori came into the back with a tray of plates. She slid them by the sink and turned to Krista. "Who's the guy?"

"A friend of Chief Cunningham," Luke said.

Krista kept working on the sandwich. She couldn't blame Luke for acting the way he did this morning. It was his job to suspect danger around every corner.

And that suspicion might keep her safe.

Tatum joined her sister in the kitchen.

"Chief Cunningham's friend," Tori explained to her sister.

Tatum walked over to the Luke and shook his hand. "I'm Tatum and this is Tori."

"Tori, can you start on the dishes?" Krista asked. "I'm not sure I've got the energy."

"Sure."

Krista finished making Luke's sandwich, garnished the plate with a pickle and a few olives and put a mini scoop of fruit salad in a dish. She placed it in front of him.

"How much?" he said.

"On the house."

He glanced into her eyes. "I can't do that."

"Why not?" Krista asked.

"It's freeloading. Let me at least do the dishes after I eat."

"Great idea!" Tori said, drying her hands and rushing off into the dining room.

"No, really I couldn't—"

"Sure she could," Tatum said, putting her arm around Krista's shoulder. "In case you haven't noticed, she has a hard time accepting help from people."

"Wise guy," Krista said.

"It's true." Tatum smiled and breezed out of the kitchen.

"Nice kids," Luke said.

"They consider me their auntie."

"Well, Auntie, I'd really like to do your dishes in exchange for lunch. And anything else I can do to help, just say the word. Okay?"

"Sure."

Krista went to clean up the stainless steel prep counter. Her insides warmed at the thought of how nice it was to have a man care about her.

Then she reminded herself he was here for work,

and part of his job required him to stick close and catch whoever was working in tandem with the drug cartel.

She rinsed off the prep table with bleach water and started on the dishes.

"Hey, hey, that's my job," Luke said.

"I'll leave some for you, no worries."

The back door opened and Alan stepped into the kitchen. He glared at Luke. "You're still here?"

"I work here."

"Yeah, right." He turned his back to Luke and went to Krista. "Hey, I wanted to make sure you were doing okay."

He touched her arm and she tried not to recoil. Alan wasn't a bad guy, just not a guy she wanted touching her. She knew he wanted more than she had to give him, and she didn't want to encourage the affection.

"I'm fine, thanks."

"Really? Because I was worried this morning."

"Thanks, just tired." She stepped away from him and rearranged the tea jars. Maybe if she kept her distance he'd get the message.

She didn't want to be rude, but she wasn't sure how to handle this situation. She'd been clear with him months ago that she wasn't interested, that she wasn't ready to get serious. With anybody.

Which wasn't exactly true. If she found the right man, a Christian man as devoted to God as he was to Krista, well, she'd definitely consider. Only there weren't a lot of single guys of her generation left in Wentworth.

Most of her classmates had gone off to college, landed important jobs in the city and didn't return home.

"Business run smoothly this morning?" Alan asked, eyeing the tables out front.

"Sure, why?" she asked.

"It's your first day back and you've got to be exhausted. I mean with your long travel day and early morning…"

God give me patience.

If he kept reminding her how tired she was, she was going to pass out right here on the hardwood floor.

She turned to him. "I'm fine, Alan, really. And I appreciate your concern. Now, if you don't mind, I'm going to finish up these dishes, so I can close early this afternoon."

She smiled brightly and hoped she'd been nice about her obvious attempt to kick him out of her space.

"I'll check on you tonight." He reached out to touch her shoulder.

"Great, thanks."

The phone rang, saving her from having to rudely pull away.

She sidestepped Alan to answer the phone. "Grace's Tea Shop."

"Yes, this is Thunder Travel Tour. We're bringing a bus through Wentworth and would like to book your restaurant for a high tea."

"Great, what's the date?"

As she took the order, she spied Alan hovering over Luke as he ate his sandwich. What was Alan's problem?

One, she and Alan weren't dating, and two, Luke wasn't interested in Krista that way.

As if he heard her, Luke glanced at Krista.

She snapped her attention to her reservation book. "That date looks good. How many?"

"Twenty-six."

"We offer a set menu for that number. Would you like me to e-mail it to you?"

"That would be great."

Krista spied Alan hovering by the doorway as if he wasn't leaving without saying a proper goodbye. As she finished the call with the travel agency, she wondered if she needed to be more direct with Alan so he could move on and find another woman to date.

"I look forward to working with you," Krista said and hung up.

Alan took a step toward her just as Tatum rushed into the kitchen. "A group of eight just walked in for high tea."

"Now?" Krista checked her watch. "We didn't have a reservation." It was nearing three, which meant Krista wouldn't be closing up anytime soon.

"No reservation, but they hoped we'd have an opening."

Krista nibbled at her lower lip. She was exhausted.

"Tell them you're booked," Alan offered.

Krista looked at Tatum. "Tell them we'll have a table ready in fifteen minutes."

Tatum nodded and went into the dining room.

"Krista, you're obviously exhausted," Alan said.

"It's all part of running my own business." She opened the refrigerator and pulled out spreads to get working on the tea sandwiches. "Thanks for stopping by, Alan."

He must have heard the dismissal in her tone. She'd been pleasant enough, and hoped he'd take his cue to leave.

"I'll call you later," he said.

With a nod, she focused on the sandwiches. A minute later she heard the door close and she breathed a sigh of relief.

Luke walked behind her to the sink. "Eight is a big order. Sure you're up to it?"

She eyed him. "What is with everybody today? I'm a big girl and I know my limitations," she said a little more firmly than she'd intended.

Luke put up his hands. "Didn't mean to offend."

"You've got a sink full of dishes."

"So I do." He turned and got to work.

Krista was exhausted by the end of the day and looking forward to a nice, quiet evening.

Instead, she came home to a crowded house full of friends who'd orchestrated an official welcome-home party.

As she stood in her living room surrounded by friends she felt so full, so at peace. Yet a part of her had hoped for quiet time to upload more photos to her blog, and maybe even sneak in that long bath she'd been fantasizing about.

She should have known something was up when the Sass girls offered to close the shop. They always had friends to catch up with after work, and church activities to attend, yet today they practically forced Krista out the back door so they could clean up.

They'd all been in on the plan: the Sass twins, Natalie and friends from church. Their goal was to show her how much she'd been missed.

"Krista?" Luke said.

She turned to him. He seemed completely out of place and more than a little uncomfortable surrounded by these down-to-earth folks.

"Looks like you're okay here so I'm going to meet up with the chief for an hour," he said.

"Oh, okay, sure."

"Hang in there." He smiled.

She realized he was the only person in the room who saw through her smile and knew how tired she really was.

"Thanks. And thanks for being my busboy today."

"Maybe you'll promote me to handyman?"

"We'll see."

"Enjoy yourself." He made his way through the crowded living room and practically ran out the front door. She wondered what made him so uneasy about the group. Was it simply that the suspect could be among them? No, she wouldn't accept that possibility.

Natalie weaved her way through the crowd. "Did we surprise you?"

"Totally."

Natalie put her arm around Krista and gave her a squeeze. "I know you're tired, but they insisted."

Krista glanced around the room and spotted Tori and Tatum's mom, Julie Sass, chatting with the youth minister.

"I should have known something was up when the Sass girls offered to close."

"Yeah, why's that?" Natalie asked.

"They've always been nervous about locking up and setting the alarm."

Natalie scanned the room. "Where's Alan?"

"He doesn't like to share me."

Natalie snapped her attention to Krista.

"Sorry, that was mean," Krista said.

"No, it was accurate. I didn't think you noticed."

"I notice a lot. I just keep it to myself."

Like she noticed how Luke bolted from the party as soon as possible. He acted as if being around friendships and laughter physically pained him. Maybe even terrified him.

Her cell vibrated on her hip. It was a text message alerting her that something tripped the alarm at the tea shop.

"Drat. The girls must be having trouble setting the alarm. I've gotta buzz over there for a minute."

"You can't go," Natalie said. "It's your party."

"It will take five minutes."

"Then I'll go with you. You look too tired to drive, anyway."

"Gosh, thanks." With a smile, Krista led Natalie out the front door. Within minutes they were at the shop.

"Stay here," Krista said, grabbed her keys from her purse and went to reset the alarm. The back door was open.

Why would they set the alarm before they locked up?

Panic gripped her stomach. "Tori? Tatum?" Krista called as she stepped into the shop.

No one answered. "Girls!"

She started for the stairs to the office and spotted broken glass and loose-leaf teas sprinkled on the hardwood floor. Backing up, she grabbed her cell phone from her belt and called 9-1-1.

"9-1-1 emergency."

"This is Krista—"

Someone grabbed her from behind, yanking the phone out of her hand and tossing it across the room. He had his arm around her neck and waist.

"Where is it?" he growled into her ear.

"What do you want?"

"Your purse, your money."

"Let me go!" She struggled against him, but he was too strong and about five inches taller than Krista.

Sirens wailed in the distance.

Her attacker shoved her aside and Krista lost her balance, banging her head on the counter as she fell to the floor.

She opened her eyes and spots cluttered her vision. Stunned and confused, she struggled to sit up and lost the battle. Collapsing against the floor, she focused on taking deep, slow breaths.

"Krista!" Natalie cried.

And the world faded to black.

FIVE

This couldn't be happening. He'd left her for ten minutes.

Adrenaline rushing through his body, Luke gripped the door handle ready to jump from the chief's cruiser.

Come on, come on. They couldn't get to the shop fast enough.

The chief finally pulled into the parking lot and Luke flung open his door.

"Wait for backup," the chief ordered.

Backup? Small-town law enforcement was no match for the likes of Victor Garcia.

"I got it." Luke jumped out of the chief's cruiser and bolted for the restaurant.

He reached inside his jacket and slipped out his Glock. He turned the corner to the back door and froze at the sight of Natalie kneeling over Krista.

No, he wouldn't accept it. He couldn't handle the possibility that Krista had been hurt…maybe even killed. His shoulder muscles tensed.

The chief rushed into the doorway, along with another cop.

"Natalie, what happened?" Luke demanded, rushing to Krista's side.

"Out front, some guy ran out front!" Natalie shouted.

"We'll check it out," the chief said.

"Someone call an ambulance," Natalie pleaded.

"It's on the way." Luke shoved his gun inside his jacket. Didn't want Krista opening her eyes to see Luke hovering over her brandishing a gun.

He kneeled on the other side of Krista and gently gripped her wrist to take her pulse. Her skin was cool to the touch, but her pulse was strong and steady.

Thatta girl.

He noticed a red bump on her forehead.

"What happened?" He glanced at Natalie. She was pale, looked like she was going to pass out herself.

"Natalie, breathe," Luke ordered. "Krista's going to be okay."

She had to be okay.

"Talk to me," he prompted Natalie.

She sniffled. "Something tripped the alarm and Krista thought the girls were having problems setting it, but we got here and the door was open and the... girls! Where are they?"

Krista moaned. "Why all the shouting?"

The chief kneeled beside them. "How is she?"

"She's coming around." Relief settled low in Luke's

gut. He glanced at the chief. "Natalie's worried about the girls who were working here earlier."

"I'll check upstairs and call their mom."

Krista moaned and blinked her eyes open. Luke had never seen anything more beautiful in his life.

Confusion creased her forehead. "I'm on the floor."

"That you are." He placed her hand on her stomach. He'd been holding it while taking her pulse and hadn't let go.

"What happened?" She touched her forehead where an ugly bruise was already forming.

"You don't remember?" Luke asked.

"I was at the party and then, no, it's foggy."

She automatically reached for her silver charm at her neck. He guessed it was her touchstone.

"Where are the paramedics?" Luke whispered, glancing out the back. He couldn't stand seeing her hurt like this, lying on the floor and probably suffering from a concussion.

The chief came downstairs. "The Sass girls are home, safe and sound."

"Thank God," Natalie said.

"Something tripped the alarm," Krista said. "I remember now."

Luke snapped his attention to her. "What else do you remember?"

"The floor, tea and glass everywhere."

Luke glanced over his shoulder at the tea racks. Sure enough the floor was covered with broken glass jars of tea.

"A man was here," Krista whispered.

Luke glanced at her. "Did you recognize him?"

"He grabbed me from behind and…" She closed her eyes.

Luke fought the urge to reach out and hold her hand, tell her everything was going to be okay.

Natalie took Krista's hand and squeezed it. "It's okay, Krista."

Krista opened her eyes and stared directly at Luke. She wanted something. He didn't know what.

"Is it…safe?"

"Yes. He's gone."

But they both knew what she was really asking was if this was connected to Garcia's drug business.

"Did he say anything?" Luke asked.

"He wanted my purse."

"Do you think it was the same guy who was hiding in your garage?"

"I don't know."

Two paramedics rushed into the kitchen and lay a backboard on the floor.

"I'm really okay," Krista protested.

Luke and Natalie stepped aside, letting the EMTs tend to Krista.

"Natalie, where's her purse, do you know?" Luke said.

"In my car."

With a nod, Luke went outside.

And spotted a man digging around in the front seat of the car. Gutsy. The place was swarming with emergency response personnel and he was trying to snatch the car? So much for this being a quiet tourist town.

Luke came up behind the guy, grabbed his arm and twisted it behind his back.

"Find what you're looking for?"

"Hey, what's the problem?" The guy struggled, but Luke pinned him against the car.

"The problem is you breaking into a stranger's car."

"This is my fiancée's car."

Natalie stepped out of the tea shop. "Timothy? What are you doing here?"

"You know this guy?" Luke said.

"He's my fiancé, Timothy Gaines."

Luke released Timothy.

"Who are you?" Timothy demanded as he rubbed his shoulder.

"A friend of the police chief."

With a disgruntled nod, Timothy turned to Natalie. "You okay, honey?" He gave her a brief hug, then stepped back and looked into her eyes. "I was driving by and saw your car in the lot. You left the keys in the ignition."

"I'm okay. Krista was attacked."

Luke studied the dynamic between the couple. Although they were engaged there was something awkward about their interaction. Then again, Luke would have no idea what a loving couple looked like. Dad had abandoned them when Luke was five, and Mom didn't want to complicate her life by getting involved with another man.

Out of the corner of his eye, Luke spotted the EMTs carrying Krista out of the shop.

"The chief will want to talk to both of you," Luke said, and marched to the ambulance. "Where are you taking her?"

"Westfield Clinic. If they think it's more serious they'll transfer her."

"I want to go with her," Natalie said.

"I need you to stay here and give your statement to Officer Sherman," the chief said.

"I'll follow her to the clinic," Luke said.

"Good." The chief and Luke shared a knowing look.

Krista's situation seemed to be getting more dangerous by the hour. Another reason Luke needed to stay close.

Closer than close.

The ambulance pulled away and Luke followed in his car. He'd left Krista in a house full of people, thinking she'd be safe, that no harm could possibly come to her in that environment.

His mistake. One he wouldn't make again.

But he'd been anxious to get out of there, away from the friends and church folk who surrounded her, welcomed her.

Loved her.

Something Luke hadn't experienced much in his life.

Mom tried, but Luke always sensed he'd been more of a burden than a bright spot in her life.

Sure he was. He'd been a troublemaker in school, always acting out, getting sent to the principal's office. Looking back, he realized it was anger at his life that drove him to lighting fires and stealing bikes. First abandoned by his father, then ten years later losing his mom to cancer.

Anger didn't begin to describe the war brewing inside Luke's chest as a teenager. After three years of being shuffled around in the foster care system, Luke channeled his anger into a different kind of war. The war in Iraq. At least it made him feel like he was doing something productive with all his rage.

Rage he'd buried, deep. Yet here he was, thinking about the past. A waste of energy.

He needed to focus on keeping Krista Yates safe. The image of her limp body lying on the floor reminded him of…

Karl, a good friend, who'd been just as motionless after Garcia shot him and left him to die.

In front of Luke.

Helpless. Gutted. There was no other way to describe the burn rushing to every nerve ending in Luke's body as he struggled to free himself from the duct tape to save his friend.

He'd felt almost as helpless when he'd heard dispatch radio the call from Krista's tea shop.

She was Luke's lead to the Garcia gang. Luke's only lead.

Yet something other than nailing Garcia made him rush out of the chief's car and into the tea shop.

Luke was worried, truly, genuinely worried.

About Krista.

"Not good," he whispered as he parked in the clinic's lot.

He had to shelve the compassionate feelings he was developing for Krista. It was ludicrous to even go there, to consider the thought of Luke and Krista being friends, much less anything more. She needed a nice, Christian man devoted to God and family.

Luke had given up on God a long time ago. About the time God took his mother and left Luke floundering in a foster care system that had no place for a teenager.

He'd seen enough violence and death in Iraq to further destroy any belief in a loving God.

He shook his head, snapping out of his analysis of his life and how Christ had failed him. Being around Krista brought it all to the surface. She glowed with the love she felt for God, her devotion to doing good deeds and caring for others.

That kind of energy was foreign to Luke and made him uneasy. That very uneasiness would be his constant reminder not to let this case get too personal, not to let Krista Yates get too close. Or was it that he didn't want her seeing all of his imperfections, especially the biggest one of all: that he couldn't protect the people he loved most?

He'd stay physically close but emotionally distant.

Easy for a guy like him, at least he thought so until he saw them wheeling her into the hospital.

Something knotted in his gut and he stormed ahead.

"You can't come in here, sir," Nurse Ruth Rankin said on the other side of the curtain. Ruth and her sister often visited the tea shop and it was nice to see a friendly face at the clinic. But Ruth didn't sound friendly, alarming Krista.

"I have to see her."

Luke's voice. Krista smiled, oddly relieved to hear the deep timbre through the curtain.

"Are you her boyfriend?" Nurse Rankin said.

"No, absolutely not," he said, panic edging his voice. "She's a friend. I need to make sure she's okay."

"Why don't you wait outside? The doctor will know more after the CT scan."

"Wait," Krista said. "Ruth?"

Ruth pushed aside the curtain. Luke eyed Krista, concern etching his forehead.

"Can he stay with me?" Krista said.

Ruth sighed. "Okay, but just until we take you up for the scan. I'll be right back."

Ruth disappeared and Luke stood there, waiting. For what, permission to step closer?

Krista wanted to reach for his hand, but felt it was inappropriate. Still, she wished she had someone's hand to hold on to. Mom. Gran. Someone.

A wave of loneliness washed over her. She touched the silver charm at her neck and found solace.

"How are you feeling?" Luke stepped closer, within inches of her bed.

She sensed his uneasiness. Why, because he didn't like hospitals? Or was it something else?

"My head hurts, but otherwise I'm okay," she said.

"Can you tell me exactly what happened at the tea shop?" He pulled out a small notebook.

Back to business.

"A guy grabbed me, demanded my purse, then threw me to the ground. I hit my head on the counter as I fell."

He scribbled something, then pinned her with intense blue eyes. "Why did you leave the party? What were you thinking?"

She was put off by his anger and critical tone.

"The alarm tripped and I figured the girls were having trouble setting it, so Natalie and I went to reset it. What did you expect me to do?"

"Be smarter than that."

"Excuse me?" She'd never seen this rude side of him.

He stepped closer. "You need to accept that this situation is dangerous, Krista. You have to…" His voice trailed off. He snapped his notebook shut. "Never mind."

He shoved his notebook into his jacket pocket and turned to leave.

She was physically bruised and emotionally exhausted.

She needed comforting words, not a lecture. Yet she suspected Luke's reaction had more to do with something in his past than Krista's experience today. She sensed he felt…guilty.

"Wait," she said.

He hesitated beside the curtain. A few seconds later he turned to her, his eyes guarded.

"I'm a small-town girl, Luke. I run a tea shop and attend church every Sunday and, well, stuff like this is foreign to me. I get that you deal with it every day, so you're smarter—"

"Don't. I shouldn't have said the thing about being smarter, that was…"

"Mean?"

He glanced at the floor. "Yeah, mean."

"But you said it because—" she hesitated "—you feel guilty?"

Clenching his jaw, he snapped his attention to her eyes. He leaned away from her, as if she'd exposed him.

"It's not your fault," she said. "It's not my fault either. How could I know someone really tripped the alarm? We've had problems with it for months. The girls don't set it often, so it would make sense they'd have difficulties."

"If I would have been at the house, I would have gone with you."

"We can't be together twenty-four/seven."

"We can and we will be. No arguments."

The determination in his voice surprised her.

"It's the only way I'm going to nail Garcia," he added.

Right. The case. This had nothing to do with Luke wanting to keep her safe because he cared about her. This was all about nailing the bad guy.

She studied his clenched jaw and piercing eyes. "Why is this case so important to you?"

"It's my job."

"I sense there's more to it."

He glanced down, as if he didn't want her looking too long into his eyes for fear she'd see something he desperately wanted to keep hidden.

"Luke?"

"Garcia killed my partner. In front of me."

A chill skittered down her arms.

"I'm so sorry." She reached out and touched his jacket sleeve, a natural, compassionate act. Luke glanced at her hand. She thought he might pull away.

"I've gotta call in." He stepped back, breaking the connection. "Don't go anywhere without me." With a nod, he walked out.

More like ran. From her.

Krista sensed he hadn't told many people about his partner, and she suspected Luke blamed himself for his death. But why?

She'd probably never find out. Truly, what mattered most was that he caught Garcia and closed down his business so he couldn't make money off hooking children on drugs.

Krista still couldn't believe the ugliness had permeated

the small town of Wentworth. The tourist town of not quite three thousand was known for its vacation activities, access to both White Lake and Lake Michigan and an annual summer festival. She couldn't fathom how crime had edged its way into the safe community.

But after today's break-in, she could no longer hope that her garage attacker was some teenager out for a thrill.

Now Grace's Tea Shop had been broken into, as if someone was looking for something very specific.

"The shop," she whispered, searching the chair next to her for her purse. She should call the Sass girls and ask if they'd clean up, restock the teas for tomorrow's business.

Nurse Rankin came around the corner with a clipboard in her hand. "Where's the boyfriend?" She winked.

"He's not my boyfriend."

"He sure acts like it."

"He's…" She didn't like keeping the truth from people in town, but knew that for Luke to solve the case he had to keep his identity a secret. "He's the protective type."

"Men only protect women they're interested in, honey. He's cute."

"I hadn't noticed."

"Uh-huh." Ruth placed the clipboard on the bed and pulled the gurney away from the wall.

Ruth wheeled Krista out of the emergency room to the elevator.

"I need to make a call," Krista said.

"After the scan." Ruth glanced over her shoulder. "Don't look now, but we're being stalked."

"What? Who?" Krista leaned up on her elbow and glanced over her shoulder.

Luke walked a couple of feet behind them. He shot her a comforting smile.

"That protective boyfriend of yours isn't letting you out of his sight, is he?" Ruth pushed.

"It's been a wacky twenty-four hours."

"I heard about the lavender garden sniffer and the Bender kid shooting out your windows.

"He didn't shoot out the windows. Just fired off some rounds, I guess. And tonight someone broke into the shop."

"What for? Your hazelnut scone recipe?"

"I have no idea."

"McIntyre," Luke said.

Ruth glanced over her shoulder. "Sir, you can't use a cell phone—"

"When? How many? Hang on." Luke rushed past Krista and pointed at the nurse. "Don't let her out of your sight."

SIX

Two of Garcia's suspected henchmen were spotted boarding a plane for the States.

Then who the ▮▮▮ broke into the tea shop and attacked Krista?

"Destination?" Luke asked his boss.

"Chicago, so maybe it's not related to your case."

"Chicago, Detroit, they're equidistant from Wentworth. But I'm afraid someone's already here."

"Why?"

"In addition to the attack last night, someone broke into the tea shop just now." Luke glanced across the town square where city workers were putting up Christmas decorations. Krista was attacked, nearly killed, and yet life went on as if nothing had happened.

"You think one of Garcia's men broke into the shop?"

"Can't be sure," Luke said. "If not, and it's someone from a rival drug organization, it could mean a drug war is brewing."

"Two rival groups after the same thing. But what?"

"I think her luggage is the key."

"Still missing?"

"Yes, sir."

"I'll put agents in Chicago on alert to find and tail Garcia's men once they land. Is the woman all right?"

"Says she's fine, but they're doing a CT scan to be sure."

"Ready for backup?" Agent Marks said.

"Not yet. More strangers in town will stir suspicion. I don't want to scare off the local contact. He's our best link."

"Have you gone through the list of people who went on the mission trip?"

"Was about to when the tea shop was hit." He'd been going over the list of names with the chief, flagging a few and forwarding them to the office for background checks. Then they got the call that the tea shop had been hit.

"Stick close to the girl. She's our best lead."

"Yes, sir."

He pocketed the cell phone and glanced up at the gray sky. It smelled like snow.

He hesitated before going back into the hospital, needing a minute to ground himself. Seeing Krista hurt, lying on the ground, had ripped open the old wounds. She shouldn't have gone to the tea shop, especially without him. What was she thinking?

She thought the girls were having problems setting the alarm and they needed her help.

Krista was always thinking about others, helping

others. Knowing this was her M.O., it was Luke's job to put her first, make sure she was safe and protected.

He'd take her home and set the ground rules: He was going to be her handyman whether she liked it or not. He would always be close, within arm's reach when she went into work, to make sure she was safe.

Not an easy assignment for Luke. She was bright and cheerful, even in the face of danger. He suspected she got that energy from God, something Luke had turned his back on years ago. She was lucky to have that kind of faith.

He wasn't sure he knew how to comfort a traumatized Krista, but her faith kept her strong.

"Comfort her? What are you thinking about?" he muttered.

This wasn't about Krista, the woman. It was about Krista, his lead to busting a major drug dealer. Losing his perspective could get them both hurt, or worse. Garcia showed no mercy when dealing with his enemies. He killed as easily as he ate lunch.

With that thought, he marched back into the clinic to find Krista. He wasn't sure why this woman got to him and he didn't care. He'd fight it, shove the edginess deep down so it wouldn't cloud his goal: nailing Garcia.

And getting out of Wentworth.

"I'm really fine," Krista said, as Luke walked her to his car.

He eyed her with suspicion.

"Okay, so I have a headache." She pinched her fore-finger and thumb together. "A teensy one."

"You're lucky you only have a minor concussion."

"I'm lucky you showed up when you did. That's twice now."

"You're welcome. Just so we're clear, I'm officially taking the job as your handyman and personal body-guard. No discussion."

"I'm too tired to argue."

"Good." He opened the car door.

"Krista? Krista!" Alan called, rushing across the parking lot.

"Hi, Alan."

The man ignored Luke and hugged Krista. With a sigh she pressed her cheek against his chest. Luke clenched his jaw.

"I'm fine." Krista broke the embrace. "I'm really fine."

"You need to close the shop," Alan said. "At least until this guy's caught."

"Absolutely not. If I close for a few days this time of year I might as well close up for good."

"Is it worth your life?"

"Hey," Luke warned. "No one's out to kill her."

Alan turned to Luke. "You don't know that."

"Who on earth would want to hurt this sweet woman?" Luke let slip.

"I have no idea, but twice in twenty-four hours—"

"Enough. I need to get her home to rest."

Krista was looking a little pale.

"I'll take her," Alan said, puffing out his chest.

"I've got it, thanks."

Alan blocked Luke from Krista. Luke didn't want trouble, although he was tempted to put this guy in a headlock and leave him gasping in the parking lot.

"Look, man," Luke started. "The chief will have my head if I don't do exactly what he asked. He asked me to see Krista safely home."

Luke stepped around the guy and opened the car door for Krista.

"Thanks," Krista said to Alan, then slid into the front seat. Luke shut the door and turned to Alan.

"If you know anything about someone wanting to hurt her, you'd better tell the chief."

The man's face hardened. "I don't know anything."

Luke studied the guy, his receding hairline, cold, judgmental eyes and thin lips. He fit way too many criminal profiles for Luke's taste.

"Good night." With a curt nod, Luke got behind the wheel and pulled out.

Just as he'd suspected, Alan was trying to make Krista nervous with his comment about her choosing between the tea shop and her life. What a ridiculous statement, at least for a local who knew nothing about the possible drug connection to Peace Church. It seemed to Luke that Alan's goal was to frighten Krista into giving up her business, giving up her independence, so she'd be dependent on others. On Alan, perhaps?

Now there's a manipulative way to get the girl of your dreams. Didn't take Luke long to figure out Alan had a major crush on Krista, but it was also obvious that Krista wasn't interested. At least it was obvious to Luke.

"I really appreciate this," she said.

"What, driving you home?"

"And offering to be my undercover bodyguard."

"It's nothing."

"Yeah, you haven't seen my handyman list of chores yet."

He appreciated her sense of humor when he knew she must still be rattled by tonight's assault.

"As long as you don't ask me to rewire the place. Not so good with electrical."

"How about hanging Christmas lights? The Christmas tea events start before Thanksgiving. Have to satisfy the tourists who come out here to shop for Christmas."

"Smart businesswoman."

"I try."

"That's why you won't close, even for a few days? We could wrap this thing up and you'd be—"

"I said no to Alan and I've known him for ten years. What makes you think I'm going to change my answer for you?"

"I carry a badge?"

"Not impressed, sorry." She smiled.

He snapped his gaze from her and stared hard at the tree-lined street ahead. He had to. That adorable smile threatened to make him forget why he was in Wentworth.

"So, what's the deal with Alan?" he said.

"He's a nice guy."

"But?" Luke pushed.

"But what?"

"It's obvious he likes you, a lot."

"I know." She slumped back against the seat.

"But you don't return the feelings. So, what's the problem?" Luke mentally scolded himself. He had no right asking her such a personal question. Yet a part of him wanted to know what qualities a woman like Krista looked for in a man.

"The problem is, I'm an independent woman. I know Alan's type. He'd suffocate me."

"Ah, the possessive type?"

"Possessive, protective, controlling."

"Sounds like there's a story there."

"I don't like to gossip."

Just as well, Luke didn't want her sharing personal feelings about another man. He shouldn't care.

But he did.

They pulled onto her street and a handful of cars were lined up in front of her house.

"The party's still going?" she said, with a desperate quiver to her voice.

"I doubt it. They're probably hanging around to make sure you're okay."

He pulled into the driveway and eyed the house. Light spilled out from the windows, giving it a warm and inviting glow. If only the houseful of friends would stay 24/7. The power in numbers would surely keep Krista safe.

But then these locals didn't know about the real danger threatening Krista.

Natalie rushed to the passenger side of the car and yanked open the door. "You're okay, thank God."

Krista got out of the car and Natalie gave her a hug.

"I'm fine, just a headache," Krista said.

Just a headache? He bet her head throbbed like a jackhammer pounding cement. Luke got out of the car and followed the women to the house.

Krista slowed as they approached the back porch. "Who's inside?"

"Timothy, Julie Sass and the girls and Pastor White. They're helping clean up and they wanted to make sure you were okay. Don't worry, they're not staying."

Krista sighed. "Thanks."

Natalie led Krista toward the house and Luke hesitated. "Krista?"

She turned to Luke.

"Don't forget, I'm close." He pointed to the garage.

"You could always come inside and help us clean up," Natalie said.

But he couldn't, couldn't handle being surrounded by so much love, so much compassion.

"It's okay," Krista said, touching his coat sleeve. "You've done plenty. Thanks."

Natalie looped her arm through Krista's and led her up the porch steps. As they opened the back door, cheers echoed from the house.

The door slammed on the welcoming sound, shutting

Luke out. Yet he stood there for a few seconds. He wasn't sure why.

"You got work to do." He went back to the car and got the files. He'd take them up to his room in the garage and get started on identifying connections between mission volunteers and the drug ring.

Working would keep his mind focused and his thoughts off of the beautiful Krista Yates.

Krista wasn't sure where she got the energy to open the next day, so she thanked the Lord for the much-needed strength.

She made a pot of coffee at home, threw in a couple of pieces of toast and was ready when Luke knocked at eight. She handed him a mug of coffee and piece of toast with peanut butter.

He was dressed more casually today. He'd traded his dress slacks, collared shirt and tie for jeans, a Chicago Bears sweatshirt over a black T-shirt and gym shoes. He leaned against the counter as he ate, Anastasia weaving between his legs. Luckily Luke wasn't much of a morning person either. Either that or he wasn't sleeping well in her drafty garage.

Guilt snagged her conscience.

"You warm enough up in the attic?" she asked, and took a bite of her toast.

"I'm fine."

"You sure?"

"I can take care of myself, no worries." He sipped his coffee.

"You're sleeping okay?"

"Not really."

"Because it's cold?"

"Because I'm worried about you." He dipped his toast in his coffee. "I've decided to get you a dog."

"What?"

"A watch dog will alert me if someone's outside."

"I can't have a dog. Anastasia—"

"I'll keep the dog outside with me."

"And when you leave?"

"We'll deal with that when the time comes."

"I don't need a dog."

"Everybody needs a dog."

That comment shocked her. Dogs were lovable and loyal and wonderfully innocent. She would have a dog except it would interfere with her travels and long work hours. It just wasn't fair to the pet.

Anastasia, on the other hand, was independent and low maintenance.

"You ready?" he asked, rinsing his plate and mug.

"Yeah." She grabbed her purse from the counter.

When she turned, he was standing a bit close, looking deeply into her eyes.

"You sure you're up to this?"

He acted like she was about to take the stage in front of a thousand people. He sounded like he really cared about her. She studied his bright blue eyes and caught herself. *Silly girl. He's a cop out to nail a criminal.*

"The question is, are you sure you're up to my handyman list?" she shot back.

"Already put tools in the car."

"All right, then."

He led her out of the kitchen, triple-checked the lock on the back door, and they took off. When they pulled into the tea shop parking lot she noticed her little Ford Focus parked in the corner. She'd forgotten she'd left it behind last night.

She'd tried to completely forget what happened last night, the shock of the intruder, his hard grip and verbal demand for her purse. But why? She didn't carry more than twenty dollars in there.

It wasn't a random purse snatching and you know it.

"Hey, you okay?" Luke asked, pulling up next to her car.

Great, now the guy could tell when she was sliding into the dark, scary places of her mind?

"Busy day ahead," she said and got out of the car. She didn't want to talk about any of it anymore: Garcia, the house intruder the other night, the break-in at the shop.

She wanted life to get back to normal. She approached the back door, deactivated the alarm and stuck her key in the door.

"Hang on, let me do the honors." Luke smiled and acted as if this was a polite gesture, not a protective one.

He swung the door open and stepped inside. Krista followed, her heartbeat thumping against her throat with the panic of what she'd find.

Oh, good grief, you can't be afraid of going to work.

She glanced in the direction of the tea racks. They'd been restocked with new glass jars filled with the twenty-three varieties of teas she kept on hand for customers. Someone had been busy last night. They'd cleaned up the tea and glass on the floor, found new jars upstairs and restocked everything.

She must have beamed because Luke winked at her.

"The tea fairies were here, huh?"

"It's good to have friends."

His smile faded. Reading pain in his eyes, she regretted saying the words and didn't know how to make him feel better.

"I'll pull the chairs down off tables while you work on my handyman list." Luke went into the dining area and got to work.

Krista checked the reservation book. They only had one, a table for four, which was good considering the decorating Krista wanted to get done for Christmas. Sure, some folks thought decorating a week before Thanksgiving was a little premature, but Krista couldn't get enough of Christmas and all it represented.

She put on a pot of coffee and started warming soups. There were enough frozen scones to hold her through the first rush, but she should probably bake more.

Krista checked the restaurant voice mail. There was only one message from the nearby Michigan Shores Resort, asking to reserve a table of six for their guests. They would be filling up for the holidays. The resort, run by Don and Marilyn Baker, put on fantastic events around the holidays.

Tourism kept the economy alive around here, but money wasn't the only reason Krista wanted the family tea shop to thrive. She loved offering people a place to gather and relax, share stories and laugh.

Of course, a man like Luke McIntyre would never understand that motivation. He was all business. She wondered when was the last time he laughed and what it sounded like.

"So, you got my list?" Luke said, coming up behind her.

"We'll start with decorating."

"For Christmas."

"Yep. Upstairs in the corner of the office are four boxes marked 'Christmas.'" She rubbed her hands together. "This is going to be fun."

"Bah humbug." He turned and disappeared up the stairs.

She wished she could brighten his attitude, make God and Christmas and community seem less threatening, but she guessed that would take a miracle.

"The Christmas season is upon us," she whispered with hope in her heart.

Christmas was a time for celebrating the birth of our Lord, a time to rejoice and be thankful. And Krista was thankful, for so many things.

She pulled the laptop out from the cabinet below the counter and powered up. She hadn't checked e-mail since she'd been home, not that she expected anything exciting. After all, everyone she knew lived in this small town and knew of her return, and the disastrous twenty-four hours that followed.

"Positive thoughts," she whispered.

Because it was a quiet day and Luke was here to put up the decorations, she'd sneak in a moment to upload a few more photos to her blog. She pulled the thumb drive off her keychain and inserted it into the laptop.

Luke pounded down the stairs into the kitchen with box number one. "You going to help me?"

"Yeah, in a sec. I haven't checked e-mail since I've been back and want to update my blog."

"You've got a blog?" He put the box down on the counter.

"Yep."

"You blog about your cat, right?" he teased.

"Sometimes. But mostly I try to inspire people, which is why I'm posting photos from my mission trip." She typed in "proverbsbabe3.com" and clicked Go.

"What's the three for?"

"My lucky number. It symbolizes the Trinity and there are three people in my family."

She waited for the blog to open. And waited. "I need a faster computer."

It finally popped open, but her page was blank. Then, suddenly, the image of a coffin floated across the screen.

SEVEN

"What the…?" Krista said.

Luke nudged her out of the way. "Someone broke into your account."

"How can they do that? Why would they do that?"

"Could be kids messing around." But Luke knew that possibility was slim. "Let's not assume anything until I check it out. Get me your Internet provider information and pass codes and I'll have my people look into it."

"Okay, thanks." She went upstairs to her office.

Luke knew it was safe up there because he'd checked it out when he got the box of Christmas decorations. He eyed the screen with the floating coffin. What had this woman stepped into? Now they were coming after her online?

Holiday music drifted through the shop from the corner speakers. She must have turned it on upstairs. Although it brightened most people's lives, Christmas songs were just another reminder of the things Luke never had: thoughtful gifts of love, family gatherings, turkey with cranberry sauce and stuffing.

His dad had died in a freak car accident when Luke

was only five, leaving Mom to raise him by herself. Mom could barely pay the light bill much less buy unnecessary presents for her kid. She did the best she could on her secretary's salary. For the first few years after Dad's death, their local church had provided them with holiday meals and presents from strangers.

Luke felt ashamed about needing handouts. At ten he told his mom he didn't want anything from the church people. He'd rather go without than suffer the embarrassment of kids at school knowing what he got for Christmas because, well, their families footed the bill.

He wondered if that's what drove Krista to being so independent. He'd read her background, knew about her father's murder and her mother moving to Wentworth when Krista was young.

It seemed he and Krista had more in common than Luke wanted to admit, only, Luke never found comfort in a God who took both of his parents away.

"Hey, is Natalie here?"

Luke turned to the back door. Timothy, Natalie's fiancé, stepped into the kitchen.

"I haven't seen her."

"Huh. I thought she said to meet her here at nine."

"We don't open until eleven," Luke said.

"We?" the man chuckled.

Luke didn't answer. He didn't have to explain himself to this guy.

"So you're the chief's friend from New York?" Timothy strolled into the kitchen and leaned against the counter to face Luke.

"I don't remember saying I was from New York, but yes, I'm friends with the chief."

"What's your interest in Krista?"

Luke narrowed his eyes at the guy. "Who wants to know?"

"My fiancée, actually. She can't figure out why you're always hanging around."

"The chief is worried about Krista and asked me to keep an eye on her."

"Yeah, well, there are lots of guys who would kill for that job. Why you?"

"Maybe because I'm former military and the chief trusts me to follow orders?"

Timothy nodded and glanced at the laptop. "Whoa, what happened there?"

"Either the site is down or someone broke in. Not sure yet."

"Kinda strange, all this stuff that's been happening. Someone breaks into Krista's house, the shop and now her computer?"

"A lot of action for a small town."

Timothy crossed his arms over his chest. "Yeah, ever since you showed up."

The guy was a few inches shorter than Luke but built like a wrestler. Still, Luke didn't want to get into a shoving match in the shop.

"You accusing me of something?" Luke said.

"I just don't like coincidences. And since my fiancée

is best friends with Krista, I feel protective of both of them."

"It's not me you have to worry about."

"Yeah, then who?"

"How would I know?" Luke said.

Good thing Luke left his shoulder firearm in the glove box. He'd be too tempted to threaten idiot Tim with it. Luke had left it in the car out of respect for Krista; plus, it wasn't easy hiding a firearm when you were only wearing a T-shirt and jeans.

"I think you know a lot more than you're saying." Timothy leaned closer.

Great. He really wanted a fistfight here, in the shop?

"Hey, Timothy," Krista said, breezing up to them with a file folder. "You looking for Nat?"

Timothy kept his gaze focused on Luke. "She was supposed to meet me at nine for scones."

"Huh, she didn't tell me. I usually wouldn't be here this early, but we've got to get the Christmas decorations up."

"Yeah, well, she probably had problems with that old clunker of hers."

"Wouldn't surprise me," Krista said, setting down the file.

A few seconds of silence passed. Timothy didn't move to leave. Luke didn't budge from his spot in front of the laptop. Krista glanced from Timothy to Luke and back to Timothy.

"What'd I miss?"

"Not a thing," Luke said.

"Great, then here's the information you asked about." She handed Luke the file and smiled at Timothy. "You want to help decorate?"

"Maybe another time. Natalie and I would love to help out."

"Oh, okay."

Luke heard the question in her voice.

"Take care, Krista." Timothy kissed her on the cheek and left.

Krista stood in the doorway for a minute and watched him leave. "What on earth was that about?"

"He thinks I brought trouble to town."

She snapped around, blond strands of hair breaking free from her clip and trailing down the side of her face. "That's ridiculous."

"He doesn't know me, Krista. And everything started happening when I showed up. It's logical."

"But untrue and unfair to accuse you."

"He's being protective. Nothing wrong with that."

"I wish you could tell everyone who you really are."

"Bad idea. I have a better chance of finding the drug contact in Wentworth by being as nonthreatening as possible. I'm just a guy, passing through town to visit his friend."

She planted her hands on her hips as if gearing up for an argument. She looked adorable.

He tapped the file folder to his palm. "I'm going to the car to call this in. I'll be right back."

"Good, because we have holly to hang."

"Can hardly wait."

It was bad enough that Timothy stopped by and gave Luke a hard time, but an hour later Alan made his daily appearance.

"Just checking in on my favorite girl," he said, coming in for a kiss. Krista turned her cheek.

This had to stop.

"I'm fine, Alan, truly." And she was getting really tired of people checking on her.

She'd received a phone call earlier from Mom and Lenny asking if she wanted them to fly to Michigan because they'd heard someone had broken into the house. Then Timothy stopped by, Natalie made an appearance and now Alan was thrusting himself into her life. They needed to stop suffocating her.

And she needed to focus on getting the shop ready to open for the lunch rush, which meant she had to get rid of Alan so she could finish decorating with Luke.

"I called early this morning. Didn't you get my message?" Alan asked.

"I was tired. Look, Alan, I have a lot of work to do this morning. Can we talk later?"

"How about dinner?"

Alan was a decent man and she didn't feel right dumping him abruptly, although in her mind they were never together. Out of respect for his feelings, she'd agree to have dinner.

"How about a sandwich at Ruby's Pub?" she offered.

"I was thinking we could drive into Grand Rapids for a more romantic setting."

Just then, Luke came downstairs with another box of decorations and nodded as he passed them on his way into the dining room.

"What's he doing here?" Alan scowled.

"Ruby's Pub," Krista confirmed. "I'll meet you there at seven."

"I could always stay and help decorate." He spied around the corner at Luke.

"We're almost done. Thanks anyway." She led Alan to the back door. "Go on. I'll see you later."

He turned to hug her goodbye, and the shop's phone rang, praise the Lord. "Gotta go."

She shut the door behind him and went to answer the phone. Luke came around the corner and grabbed it.

"Hello?" he said, then eyed the phone and hung up. "Wrong number."

"More like you scared them off."

"How do ya figure?"

"They call Grace's Tea Shop and a deep male voice answers 'hello'," she imitated.

"I don't really sound like that, do I?" He smiled.

In the flash of a second she realized she shared a comfortable connection with Luke that she'd never felt with other men, especially not Alan.

"What?" he said, studying her.

"Nothing, just an aha moment."

"Want to share?"

"Nope. Like to keep you guessing." She strolled into the dining room. The tree filled the corner of the shop, the holly garland was strung from the windows and photographs in holiday frames lined the mantel over the fireplace. "Looking good, handyman."

"One more box and we're done with inside work. The other two boxes are outside lights." He turned to her. "You ready for customers?"

"Yep, food prep is done. We've only got two reservations, which is good because Tatum can't get here until one."

"So you're on your own," he said.

"Unless you want to strap on an apron and help me out up front."

"Uh, I'd probably break your dainty cups."

"They're stronger than they look."

"I'll bet they are."

His blue eyes captivated her, and for a second she forgot why this man had come to Wentworth. More like, she wished it wasn't because he was a federal officer out to get a drug-dealing killer. She wished…

With a forced smile, she turned her back to him and dug into the box of decorations. She pulled out the first thing she touched: a ball of mistletoe.

Oh, boy.

"What is it?" he said.

"You've never seen mistletoe?"

"Not like that I haven't." He fingered it like a kid

fascinated by a new toy. Then his eyes caught hers. "What do you want me to do with it?"

She couldn't help but glance at his lips. Talk about awkward.

"Hang it in the doorway." She shoved it at him and turned back to the contents of the box. *Focus,* she coached herself.

Why couldn't she feel this kind of attraction to a solid, safe man like Alan? Why did a guarded man in a violent career be the one who drew her in?

Shaking off her thoughts, she pulled out a box of ornaments and opened the top. She smiled as her eyes caught on the nativity scene ornament she'd made in the fifth grade. This was possibly her favorite: the birth of baby Jesus with the star sparkling above.

"What else did you find there?" Luke said, walking up to her.

"Ornaments for the tree." She placed the nativity scene ornament on the tree front and center.

"You make that?"

"Yep. I made most of these. They're dated on the back." She pulled out another ornament, this one of a cross with the word *Faith* running vertically down the center. "Dive in."

She and Luke hung ornaments for the next few minutes as soft holiday music filled the shop.

Krista hung the Kitten in a Box ornament. "I love this time of year."

Luke kept pulling out ornaments, putting some down and looking at others.

"There's nothing here dated before 1988. Guess you weren't much of an artist before then?"

"Actually, we had to leave those ornaments behind."

"Behind? Oh, right." He placed a lighthouse ornament on the tree.

"You know, don't you?" She eyed him.

"About?"

"Me and my mom fleeing California after my dad was killed."

"I read your background file." He placed his hands on his hips. "I'm sorry I brought it up."

She shrugged. "It was a long time ago."

But they both knew it still haunted her, especially considering recent events.

"I guess you were lucky to find a home here in Wentworth," he said.

"Yep, in a safe, quiet town. At least it was until this week."

Luke stepped closer and placed his hands on her shoulders. "Things will be safe again, I promise."

"I don't even know you, yet I totally believe you. How do you do that?"

He smiled. "Charisma?"

"I guess. Okay, you know all about me. When do I get to read your background file?"

He dropped his hands to his sides. "It would put you to sleep."

"I doubt that." She bent down for another ornament. "Come on, tell me about your family."

She grabbed a foam ornament covered with sequins

and started to place it on the tree. She paused at the odd expression on Luke's face.

"It's not a hard question," she prompted. "Where did you grow up? Do you have brothers and sisters? What made you become an federal agent?"

"What, you writing an article for the local paper?" He pulled an ornament from the box and casually placed it on the tree.

Krista sensed the tension in his body. She could see it in the way he held his shoulders.

"Hey, if you're going to be my shadow until this is over I'd like to know something about you," Krista said.

Luke hung the ornament and stared her down. "All you need to know is I'm going to keep you alive."

He turned and left the dining room.

Did she hit a nerve or what? Was it possible that Luke had an even darker history than Krista?

Fine, she wouldn't push him. She felt sure that given enough time he'd open up to her. *Why is it so important to you?*

"It shouldn't be," she muttered.

But it was. Probably because of the angst she read in his eyes when he wasn't covering with bravado or humor.

Krista finished with the last of the ornaments and carried the box into the back. Luke was nowhere to be seen. Yeah, he was probably hiding in his car. Whatever. She had to respect his need to keep his life private.

He came downstairs carrying another box. "I'm goin' outside to do the lights."

She grabbed her coat and followed him out the back door.

"Don't you have scones or something to bake?" he said, as if he didn't want her around.

Whenever his curt side popped out, she couldn't decide if she should turn and walk away, point her finger in his face and give him a lecture or shower him with compassion.

She chose compassion, because that was the most Christian thing to do. She grabbed the ladder and followed him to the front of the shop.

"I'm very particular about my lights," she said.

"I'll bet you are," he joked.

So he was covering with humor again. Interesting. She leaned the ladder up against the house and shook it to make sure it was secure.

He started up the ladder with the box in his hands.

"Careful," she warned.

"You're making me nervous."

"Sorry." She gripped the ladder so it wouldn't budge.

Luke slid the box onto the asphalt shingles and climbed onto the roof. "Okay, boss, where do I start?" he asked with a smile.

"String the bigger lights along the roof line. The clips should be there from last year."

Luke kneeled down and fingered the edge of the roof.

"Okay. You want them to go all around the roof or just in the front?"

"All around, please."

"Yes, ma'am."

A car pulled into the lot with three ladies inside.

"Looks like you've got customers. I can handle this."

She hesitated.

"Go on. I won't mess up, too badly." He disappeared to the other side of the roof and she headed inside to prepare for the first customers of the day.

Shucking her coat, she tossed it on the stairs going up to the office and grabbed a few menus. She took a deep breath and greeted the three middle-aged women.

"Good morning, ladies," she said. "You have your choice of tables."

The short blonde woman with a round face pointed to the corner table by the tree and her friends followed.

"Have you ever been to Grace's Tea Shop before?" Krista asked.

"I came last year with my mom while staying at the Lakeside Resort. I'm back for a girls' weekend." She smiled at her friends.

"Sounds great. We specialize in high tea, offering three different versions."

The ladies sat down and Krista handed them menus. "We also have salads, soups and sandwiches. I'll give you a few minutes to—"

A loud bang echoed from outside, followed by pounding from the ceiling. Krista instinctively ducked and glanced out the window…

…just as Luke dropped off the roof.

EIGHT

Stunned, Luke struggled to breathe as he stared up at the gray November sky. What on earth just happened? He heard a loud crack, like a gunshot, lost his footing and tumbled off the roof.

Which meant someone was shooting at him? He had to get up, protect Krista.

He pinched his eyes shut against the frustrating paralysis of his lungs. That was the only thing he could feel right now, not the pain of a possible broken limb or concussion. He couldn't even tell where he'd been hurt. He just knew he had to have done some kind of damage in the fall.

"Luke?"

He looked up into Krista's warm green eyes. And for a second he felt a kind of peace he'd never experienced before.

Then panic set in.

"Got to…" He struggled for air to form the rest of his sentence. He had to get up, get her inside where it was safe.

"Don't move. An ambulance is on the way."

"No," he gasped. "Can't leave you."

"Don't argue with me or…or I'll fire you." She shot him a stern look and placed her hand to his chest.

Her touch made him relax, helped him focus. Should he tell her he'd been shot at? And that they could be aiming for her next?

No, it made no sense to kill Krista. Abduct her, maybe, but not kill her. She had something Garcia's men wanted. She'd be no good to them dead.

He got it together, took a deep breath. "You need to get inside."

The squeal of a siren echoed across the parking lot. "Help is here. Everything's going to be fine."

He didn't believe it, wouldn't believe it until he nailed Garcia and got this woman out of danger.

"Over here!" she called out.

A second later Officer West came into view.

"I was a block away when I heard your call. What happened?" Officer West asked.

"I heard a bang—"

"It sounded like a gunshot," Luke interrupted Krista.

With a nod, Officer West took a few steps away and spoke low into her radio.

Luke tried to push himself up, but Krista wasn't having any of it.

"Don't you dare move," she ordered. "The cops are here, the ambulance is coming. You just stay put."

"I'm fine." In truth he had no idea how fine he was until he stood up. "Get inside. You've got customers."

"They'll wait. You think that bang was a gunshot?"

"It sounded like it. I ducked, but lost my footing."

She glanced nervously over her shoulder. "Where is that ambulance?"

"Krista?"

She glanced at him. "I never should have asked you to put up my lights."

"Stop, this is not your fault." He placed his hand over hers. But he could tell she didn't believe him. "Help me up."

"I will not."

"Fine, then I'll get up by myself."

With a fortifying breath, he pushed off the ground and stood, wavering slightly against pain in his left ankle. Krista grabbed his arm for support.

"Hey, wait for the ambulance," Officer West said as the ambulance pulled into the parking lot.

"I don't need paramedics."

"Stop being a jerk and let them take a look at you," Krista argued.

"Is than an order, boss?"

"Yes, it is." She waved the EMTs over.

Luke didn't know any other way to deal with this situation than to try and lighten the mood. Deep down he was worried that if someone was bold enough to shoot at him in public, who knows what they'd do next.

To Krista.

Two EMTs rolled a stretcher over to the sidewalk.

"I don't need that." Luke started for the ambulance and Krista wouldn't leave his side. He wished she'd go into the shop, although he felt they were pretty safe out here with the cops and emergency crews swarming the lot. The perp would be a fool to take another shot at him.

If someone was shooting at him, that meant he'd blown his cover.

Clenching his jaw against the pain, he hobbled to the ambulance. It wouldn't hurt to let them get a look at his ankle, maybe wrap it for support.

He sat on the edge of the ambulance. "I'm not going to the hospital."

The younger EMT glanced at Krista. She shook her head. "He's a grown man. We can't force him."

"Sir, where are you hurt?" an older guy, with jet-black hair asked.

"My ankle." He stretched it out and winced.

"Okay, sir. We're going to check your vitals and your eyes for signs of a concussion."

Krista stayed close, nibbled at her fingernail. She looked worried, truly concerned about Luke's well-being. Sure she was. He was her only protection against Garcia.

"Krista!" Alan called from behind her.

She didn't budge from her spot next to Luke.

"Krista, what happened?" Alan nudged his way beside Krista.

"I fell off the roof," Luke said. He made eye contact with Krista and a silent understanding passed between them. He didn't want to discuss the shooting with just anybody. At this point Luke wanted to keep it between the chief, Officer West, Luke and Krista.

"Thank goodness you're okay," Alan said to Krista and pulled her aside.

Luke wanted her to stay close where he could keep an eye on her. Yeah, like he'd be able to protect her in his condition?

The older EMT checked his blood pressure, flashed a light in his eyes and then got a look at his ankle.

"Will I live?" Luke said.

"The ankle is definitely sprained, but I can't tell you if it's broken until you get an X-ray." The guy straightened. "You probably have a concussion. You were lucky you landed on the pile of broken-down boxes."

Luke glanced across the parking lot. He was lucky it was recycling day and the shop's delivery boxes were stacked and laying just right to break Luke's fall.

"You sure we can't convince you to take a ride?" the EMT encouraged.

"No, thanks anyway."

"We'll wrap the ankle. Get crutches and stay off it for a couple of days," the younger EMT said.

"Will do."

Luke watched Krista and Alan across the parking lot as the younger EMT wrapped his ankle. He hated weakness of any kind, especially physical weakness. He had no intention of using crutches. It would make him look weak, vulnerable.

Luke stepped away from the ambulance, clenching

his jaw against the pain. Officer West stepped up to him. "Need a hand?"

"I'm good, thanks."

Officer West glanced across the parking lot at Alan who was in a heated discussion with Krista. "That guy creeps me out."

"What do you know about him?"

"He moved here a few years ago to get away from the city. I guess he's some kind of techno geek. He's dense, that's for sure. I mean she obviously isn't interested."

Chief Cunningham pulled up and got out of his cruiser. "What in the name of sweet peaches happened here?"

Luke motioned him closer. "I heard what sounded like a gunshot and lost my footing. Fell off the roof."

The ambulance pulled out.

"Shouldn't you be going with them?" the chief asked.

"He's stubborn," Officer West said.

"Do I have to pull rank?" the chief threatened.

"Thanks for the concern, sir, but I'm really okay," Luke said. "Just a sprained ankle."

"Lucky you," the chief said. "Officer West, canvass the area and determine if anyone else heard anything resembling a gunshot."

"You don't believe me?" Luke said.

"I believe you, son. But let's rule out other possibilities first. There's construction on the north end of town, and the local mechanic could be working on a stubborn car. We'll do a canvass just to be sure."

"I'll radio in, sir." Officer West got in her patrol car and took off.

"Anything else you can tell me?" the chief said.

"No, sir."

"Okay, then get inside and ice that ankle before it blows up like a hot air balloon." He glanced across the parking lot. "Krista!"

She sidestepped Alan and rushed over to Luke and the chief. "Thanks, chief," she whispered.

The chief eyed Alan, who hovered in the parking lot for a minute before getting into his car.

"Take Luke inside and make him ice that ankle. I'll bring some crutches by later."

"I don't need crutches," Luke said.

"Yes, you do," Krista said, leading him to the back of the shop. She frowned and Luke eyed her.

"The chief thinks the sound could have been a car backfiring," Luke offered, hoping it would ease her concern. But he wasn't letting his guard down.

"It's not that." She got him set up at the employee break table in the back.

"What, boyfriend trouble?" He shifted into the chair with a groan.

"He's not my boyfriend." She scooped cubes into a dish towel. "I'd planned to clear things up with Alan tonight at dinner, but I can't leave you in this condition."

"It's a sprained ankle, Krista. I'll live. But I don't want you going anywhere without me."

"Three's a crowd, or haven't you heard?" She pulled out a second chair and she placed his foot on it.

She gently adjusted the ice pack to his ankle and he clenched his jaw against the cold.

"Don't worry about it," she said. "I need to make sure you take it easy."

He started to argue with her, then realized if a guilt trip kept her from running off to meet Alan, then Luke would go along.

He'd use whatever means necessary to keep her close and out of danger.

"Stop fretting." He motioned her to back off. "You've got customers."

"But you'll—"

"Stop babying me or I'll climb back on the roof and finish the lights."

"You wouldn't dare."

"Try me." He smiled.

"Okay, message received." With a shake of her head, she grabbed an order pad and disappeared into the dining room.

He pulled out his cell. If someone had been shooting at him that meant the threat was already here.

Only, why couldn't they see it? Especially the locals? The chief seemed pretty sharp and on top of his game. He'd have to know about strangers in town.

Unless Garcia had enlisted the help of a local, someone that no one would suspect, someone they all trusted as one of their own. Luke needed the folder of names and background information he'd left in the car.

His foot was pounding and his head still buzzed from the fall, but he couldn't just sit here doing nothing. He grabbed the ice pack and placed it on the table. Pushing the chair back, he lowered his foot and started to get up.

"Don't even think about it," Krista said, walking into the kitchen. "You're staying put if I have to duct tape you to the chair."

The man was impossible. It was bad enough Krista had to run the shop single-handedly, but she also had to play babysitter to a stubborn federal agent who was cranky as anything.

But he was alive.

She sighed at the thought as she spread dilled cream cheese on a slice of bread. If he'd fallen differently off the roof…

No, she wouldn't go there. Things happened for a reason. Luke's job wasn't finished here in Wentworth. He was meant to survive the fall and close his case.

And make her life miserable in the process.

"I hate to bother you, but—"

"Give me two minutes," Krista interrupted him, wanting to put the finishing touches on the tea sandwich.

"I'm leaking," Luke said.

She turned to see a puddle forming on the hardwood floor.

"Shoot." She dropped the knife and rushed to him. She kneeled beside the chair and gently removed the ice pack. "I'm sorry."

"It's not your fault."

Just then, Tatum Sass waltzed into the back of the shop. "Whoa, did I interrupt something?"

"Just the first lunch rush," Krista said, racing across the kitchen to dump the towel in the sink.

"What happened to him?" Tatum asked.

"Fell off the roof," Luke said.

"What were you doing on the roof?"

"Hanging lights," Krista answered. "Which means I'm going to have to finish hanging them tonight after work."

"Oh, no, you're not," Luke argued.

"Boy, you guys sound like Tori and her old boyfriend. Argued all the time." Tatum hung up her jacket and grabbed an apron. "Status out front?"

Krista put on a new pair of gloves and went back to working on tea sandwiches. "You need to take a food order for table five, table three is waiting on the Duchess's Tea and table two is ready for a check."

"Check," Tatum joked.

"Go on, get out there. This order will be ready in five." Krista nodded at the three-tiered tower that was waiting for sandwiches, fruit and scones.

"Oh, and he needs more ice for his ankle," Krista said. "Can you do that first?"

"No," Luke protested. "It's better. Go on and take care of customers."

Tatum shrugged and went out into the dining room.

"It only would have taken her a minute," Krista said over her shoulder.

"Don't make me feel guilty about you neglecting your customers on my account."

"Why not? I already feel guilty about your injury."

"Stop, or I'm going to get my own ice."

She turned to him. "Don't you dare."

"Then stop worrying about me." He smiled and went back to studying the contents of his folder. A folder he wouldn't let Krista get from his car because he wouldn't let her out of his sight.

So he'd called the chief who'd sent Deanna West back to get Luke's keys and retrieve the folder. He'd been engrossed in the contents, jotting down notes and flipping pages for the past three hours.

When Krista slid a cup of soup and a sandwich in front of him, he'd barely noticed but managed to grunt out a "thanks." He was absorbed all right. She wished she knew what was so fascinating, but simply didn't have time to ask.

The second rush hit just about the time Tatum showed up. Thanks goodness for the teenager's arrival, and her efficiency.

Someone tapped on the back door. Good grief, if it was Alan again she was going to lose it. He'd called her every hour to make sure she was okay.

Instead, Chief Cunningham stepped into the kitchen. He nodded at Krista.

"Hey, chief," Krista said. "Need some lunch?"

"No, no, just stopped by to bring some crutches for gimp here." The chief offered the crutches to Luke.

"Thanks." Luke pushed the chair aside and stood on one foot, adjusting the crutches under each arm.

"Should fit about right. My son broke his leg a few years ago. He's about your height." He motioned to the door. "You mind giving those a spin outside?"

Krista didn't miss the chief's subtle nod. She suspected he had news about the case and didn't want anyone overhearing. Still, Krista should be kept in the loop, shouldn't she?

Luke glanced at Krista. "I'll be right back."

Another group of four wandered into the shop, keeping Krista distracted from the goings-on outside. A good thing. Although she wanted to know what was happening with the case, and if someone had really taken a shot at Luke, she had to stay on top of her game if she was to serve customers.

Making delicious food presented in a beautiful manner, served in a charming setting was her ministry in life. Just like catching criminals was Luke's.

She wondered how many drug dealers or murderers he'd put away in his career as a federal agent. Well, she thanked God for people like Luke, men who were dedicated to justice and protecting innocent people.

She also thanked God for bringing Luke into her life at this tumultuous time. She realized that after knowing him only briefly, she'd miss him when this was over: his surly nature, teasing tone and protective attitude. But that was the way of things. It's not like she could ever have a relationship with a man who thrived on the rush of violence. She'd had enough violence in her life, thank you very much.

And once this drug-smuggling case was closed, she hoped to go back to her old, normal life. She sighed as relief washed over her. Or was it melancholy?

As she and Tatum cleaned up at the end of the day, Krista puzzled over Luke's mood. The chief had told him that the gunshot sound was actually a car's backfire. Dispatch received four calls about the same time Luke fell off the roof.

Luke didn't seem convinced.

"Dining room's done, sinks and coffeemaker are rinsed," Tatum said, planting her hands on her hips, waiting for orders.

"Then we're good." Krista untied her apron. "Not bad for just two of us."

"Cool." Tatum pulled out her cell phone. "And it's only four. Awesome. I've got plenty of time before my date."

"Gabe again?"

Tatum smiled. "Yup. Pizza and a movie in Muskegon."

"A movie." Krista leaned against the counter. "I haven't seen one of those in ages."

"I'll let you know if it's any good." Tatum grabbed her jacket and stepped into the doorway. "It's a romantic comedy called *Sugar and Spies*."

"The kid must really like you to sit through a chick flick," Luke interjected, closing his folder and leaning against the table to stand.

Krista rushed over to assist, but he put out his hand to stop her. She tried not to feel offended. Why wouldn't he accept her help?

"Bye, guys." Tatum breezed out the back.

"So, you hungry?" Krista said.

"Got a stop to make first."

"Where?"

"Surprise. You want to drive?"

He must be in more pain than he was letting on.

"Sure. Your car or mine?"

"Mine, if that's okay." Using the crutches, he managed his way to the door and scanned the surrounding buildings.

Krista set the alarm and locked up. "Where are we going?"

"The pound."

"But I can't have—"

"Look," Luke interrupted. "I've made up my mind on this. We could use the added security at your house."

It did no good to argue with him. The man was determined to get her a watch dog.

Wentworth didn't have a pound, so they ended up at an animal shelter one county over where, of course, she wanted to rescue all of the twenty-plus dogs barking and shivering and begging to go home with someone.

That is why she avoided these places. She couldn't stand the pain of seeing abandoned animals. She hugged her midsection and glanced down the center aisle at the poor creatures, God's creatures.

Luke touched her arm. "This upsets you. I'm sorry."

She shrugged. Luke placed his forefinger and thumb to her chin and lifted her gaze to meet his. "Look at it this way, we're saving one of these dogs tonight, right?"

She nodded. "But how do you choose?"

Luke scanned the row of barking dogs and a slow smile curved his lips. "That's him." He pointed his crutch at a barrel-chested, big white dog with a small, black-and-white head.

"Why him?"

"He's stubborn, he's a survivor. I can tell."

Krista wondered if Luke was describing the dog or himself. She wondered what else Luke had survived and how he'd managed to make it without the comforting hand of Jesus.

"What's his name?" she said.

They ambled toward the black-and-white dog.

Luke tilted his head to read the chart. "Roscoe." Luke leaned his crutches against the cage and kneeled down. "You wanna come home with me, buddy?"

Roscoe crouched low and barked, wagging his tail.

They checked out quickly thanks to Luke's federal ID. Krista suspected there would usually be a lot more paperwork and screening involved to make sure the people adopting the pet were qualified.

An hour later they pulled up at Krista's house. Luke and Roscoe headed for the garage. "Wanna check out your new home, buddy?"

Suddenly it dawned on Krista that Luke would have to manage the loft stairs on crutches. He must have read regret on her face.

"What?" he said. "I told you I'd keep him in the garage with me."

"The stairs."

"What about them?"

"Your crutches."

"Enough already. You need to stop worrying about me. Now, come on, help us get set up in the garage."

Krista couldn't stop worrying. She moved boxes around to make room for the dog kennel, and stacked more wood for the stove in case it turned bitter cold. Sure, the garage was heated, but it never seemed to get as warm as the house because of the peaked roof.

She was on her way back in with a pile of wood when something dropped from the loft. She shrieked and jumped back. Luke had tossed the mattress over the railing.

"You're going to freeze down here," Krista said.

"First you don't want me doing the stairs, now you don't want me sleeping down here."

He was right, everything coming out of her mouth sounded like an argument. She couldn't help it. She was worried about Luke, and more than she should be for a man just doing his job.

As she built a hearty fire, he came up behind her and touched her shoulder.

"Hey, relax for a second." He led her toward the stairs with a hand to the small of her back.

His hand felt warm and solid against her body, not itchy like whenever Alan touched her.

Alan. Drat.

"What time is it?" She pulled out her cell phone. It was only six.

"You late?"

"I told you, I had a dinner date, but I'm not going," she said, cutting off his protest. "Still, I need to call Alan."

Luke adjusted himself on the stairs and patted his leg. "Come here, buddy." Roscoe trotted over to him.

Krista walked to the doorway and made her call. Alan's voice mail picked up and she breathed a sigh of relief. It wasn't going to be easy letting him down.

"Hey, Alan, it's Krista. I'm sorry but we're going to have to reschedule dinner. I ran into a problem tonight." She glanced at Luke, who studied her with intense blue eyes. "But everything's okay, no worries." She turned away from Luke. "Call me and we'll figure out another time. Thanks. And I really am sorry."

She slipped her phone into her pocket.

"So, I'm a conflict?" Luke raised a brow.

"Well, it is a problem that you're hurt and need some-one to look after you and since there's no one else in town—"

"I don't need looking after, but I don't want you going out with that guy alone, either."

"Come on, Alan's harmless."

"That's debatable." He narrowed his eyes at her.

"Even so, you and I are joined at the hip, remember? At least until this case is closed."

"And then you're gone, off to save some other damsel in distress." She smiled at him.

Luke wasn't smiling. He clenched his jaw and his blue eyes darkened. Her heart raced at his intense expression.

With a tennis ball in his mouth, Roscoe nudged Luke's knee to play.

Luke broke eye contact and she had to remind herself to breathe. What had just happened?

"Where'd you get that, buddy?" Luke said.

"We've got all kinds of treasures in here," Krista recovered. "Boxes and boxes of family stuff."

Luke glanced at the shelves stuffed with boxes marked by year. Mom and Gran kept nearly every art project, every handmade Christmas ornament, Mother's Day projects and birthday presents Krista made them.

"I'm envious." Luke patted Roscoe's furry mane. "I mean, to have this kind of history of your life, to have family and friends."

"Surely you have friends."

"Had one."

She suspected his one friend was the partner who was killed by Victor Garcia. She said a silent prayer to the Lord to help open Luke's heart to people again.

To risk loving again.

"Brothers and sisters?" she tentatively asked.

"Nope, just me."

"What about your parents?"

Luke snapped his attention to her and her breath caught at the pain in his eyes. She wanted to reach out, touch his cheek and tell him everything was going to be okay.

How crazy was that?

She glanced at his lips, just for a second, and found herself wanting to kiss him to warm the chill from his eyes.

"Krista," he whispered.

Did he sense her thoughts? Would he…kiss her? She'd kissed a few other men, sure, but never a man like this, a broken warrior bent on exacting justice.

Suddenly a low, menacing growl rumbled in Roscoe's throat.

NINE

Luke grabbed Roscoe's collar so he wouldn't bolt, and leaned close to Krista. "Take Roscoe and hide under the stairs until I tell you to come out," he whispered. He inhaled her floral scent, so incongruous to the danger hovering outside the garage.

"But—"

He placed his forefinger to her lips. Not a good idea.

"Go on," he ordered.

She nodded and led the dog beneath the stairs. Once they were out of sight, Luke slipped his off-duty revolver from his ankle and started for the door.

He didn't like waving a gun around in Krista's presence. It upset her and the look in her eye made him feel like a monster.

Luke hobbled out of the garage into the night, barely noticing the pain of a sprained ankle thanks to the adrenaline rush. The chill cleared his focus and he made his way along the side of the house to the front.

The sound of pounding made him hesitate. Someone was trying to break into her house in the front.

Luke turned the corner and aimed his firearm at a tall, skinny guy, mid-twenties with spiked red hair.

"Freeze!" Luke ordered.

"Don't shoot!" The guy stumbled backward.

Luke flashed his badge. "I'm a cop. Who are you?"

"Flower delivery for…for…" He looked at the gift card. "For Krista Yates."

"Bring it down here."

With a nervous nod, the guy walked down the stairs toward Luke.

"ID," Luke said.

The guy blinked, staring at Luke's gun.

"Put the flowers down and show me some ID."

With trembling hands, the guy put the flowers on the ground and pulled out his wallet. His license read Brent Baker of Wentworth.

"Hands against the porch, Brent," Luke said. He wasn't taking any chances.

Brent turned around and grabbed the porch railing. Luke shoved the gun into the waistband of his jeans and patted down Brent. He didn't find a firearm, but found a multifunctional pocketknife clipped to his belt.

Luke snapped it off and waved it in the guy's face.

"Come on, man, everyone's got one of those," Brent protested.

"Luke?"

Luke snapped his attention to Krista who was peeking around the house.

"I told you to stay in the garage," Luke snapped.

Brent took a few steps away from Luke.

"Where are you going, kid?" Luke said.

The guy put his hands out. "I don't need a tip, it's fine, really, it's okay."

The guy stared at Luke's gun, tucked in his waist-band, then glanced up at Luke, terrified.

Luke was losing it, suspecting everyone and their sisters of being involved in the Garcia conspiracy. Brent was an innocent kid who'd crossed paths with a crabby agent thanks to a sprained ankle and lack of sleep.

"Sorry." Luke pulled a five-dollar bill from his wallet and handed it to the guy. Brent took another step back.

"Go on, take it," Luke said as pleasantly as he could.

Brent dodged forward, snatched it and ran. He jumped in his van and peeled out.

"Your knife!" Luke called after him. But he was halfway down the block. Luke slipped the knife into his jeans pocket.

"What's this?" Krista approached Luke, Roscoe following close behind. She kneeled beside the flowers and pulled the card from the outside of the package.

"Hang on, let me check it out first," Luke said.

She looked up and smiled. "You're kidding, right?"

"No, ma'am."

"It's just flowers." Her expression was a cross between disbelief and anger.

"We can't be too careful—"

"Okay, fine. Take it." She shoved the card at his chest and went around back.

He couldn't blame her for being upset. Her life had been turned upside down and crooked, all because she'd gone on the mission trip, done something selfless and good, without expecting anything in return.

She certainly didn't expect danger to follow her back to Wentworth.

Luke picked up the flowers and hobbled around to the back porch. The mutt pranced beside him. "Good boy, Roscoe."

The dog had done his job, alerting them to potential danger.

Luke sat on the back porch and put his weapon back in his ankle holster. He carefully unwrapped the flowers to reveal a colorful bouquet in a glass jar with a red ribbon. He fingered the card feeling a bit like a jerk, but he had to be suspicious of everything and everyone.

Except Krista. Her innocence and compassion was the only truth he knew for sure. That, and he wouldn't let anyone hurt her.

He ripped open the card. It read: Looking forward to tonight. Love, Alan.

Love? Did the guy really think she loved him when it was painfully obvious she didn't have strong feelings for the guy?

He shoved the note into the envelope and blew out a slow, deep breath. Alan definitely knew what he wanted and wasn't giving up.

Well, that made two of them. Luke wasn't going to let Garcia's men get to Krista. So Alan and Luke had something in common: They both cared about Krista.

Cared about her? *Only in relation to the case, buddy. Don't lose your head.*

Luke stood, picked up the flowers and started for the back door. The adrenaline rush from their unexpected visitor had worn off, and the ankle pain was back, irritating him, making him feel weak and dependent. He tapped on the glass window of the back door with his knuckles.

Krista took her time answering. When she finally opened the door she wouldn't look at him.

"I'm sorry," he said. He hadn't a clue how those words slipped out. "The flowers are fine. I wish I could say they're from me." He joked, holding them out to her.

She took them and went into the kitchen. "Who are they from?" She turned to him. "You read the card, right?"

"Alan," he said.

She shook her head. "Oh, boy."

With a burst of excitement, Roscoe bolted past Luke into the kitchen.

"Roscoe, no!" Luke lunged for the dog and tripped on the threshold, grabbing for a chair, table, anything as he went down. Instead, he completely lost his balance and hit the kitchen floor with a thud.

Lying flat on his back, humiliation flooded his chest. Then the dog rushed him and started licking his face.

"Enough!" Luke said, grabbing him by the collar.

Luke scrambled to get control of the situation, pushing the dog away with one hand, while trying to sit up against the wall. It was more of a struggle than it should have been, and he was breathing heavily by the time he got control of things.

"Sit!" he ordered. Roscoe obeyed, his tongue hanging out, ready for more action.

Krista closed the back door and put her hand to her lips, covering up a smile that made her green eyes sparkle.

"What's so funny?" he said, with more edge than necessary. But he didn't like being out of control, looking like a fool.

"Sorry, you just, for a second you seemed like—"

"What, stupid?"

"No, human."

Which meant she thought him nonhuman before?

"Wait, that's not the right word," she corrected, kneeling beside him. She pinned him with her green eyes and he couldn't look away. "I guess the word is relaxed, laid-back, you know, not so uptight." She smiled, and he found himself wanting to brush his thumb across her lips to absorb her warmth. The thought created an ache in his chest for something he thought cold and dead.

"How about dinner?" She stood, breaking the spell.

"I should take Roscoe outside."

"No, I can gate off the kitchen so he won't terrorize Anastasia."

"Are you sure it won't be the other way around?"

"Very funny." She pulled an expandable gate from the pantry and set it up between the living room and kitchen.

"That should work." She pulled out a pot and filled it with water.

"Hang on, you've been cooking all day," Luke protested.

"I still have to cook for myself. Besides, I don't think it's a great idea for you to be standing at the stove, do you?"

"Guess not."

"What time did you take your last pain reliever?"

"Why, do I look that bad?"

"You do that a lot." She turned on the gas burner.

"What?"

"Avoid the question with a question."

"I'm used to asking questions, not answering them."

"No kidding."

He didn't miss the sarcasm in her voice.

"One-thirty," he answered.

"Five hours ago. You're due. I'll get the ice first."

She filled a dish towel with ice and put it in a plastic bag.

"Try not to leak this time." She winked and shifted the ice bag in place, studying his expression, probably to determine if she was hurting him.

He snapped his attention from her brilliant green eyes to his ankle, where she carefully adjusted the ice pack. He couldn't stand much more of this, her tending to him, icing his injury, making him dinner. It made him...edgy.

"What else can I get you?" she said, sounding like

she really cared, like her goal in life was to take care of Luke.

He wanted her out of his space. Out of his head.

"You've done enough." He stared at the ice pack.

"Okay." She went to the stove and got out another pot. "Spaghetti sound good?"

"Anything's fine." He really needed to get out of here and away from the illusion of a woman cooking for him, nurturing him.

Loving him.

It wasn't real. It was all part of the job.

Her cell phone rang from her coat pocket and she glared at it.

"Not answering it?" Luke asked.

"It's probably Alan. This is going to be messy."

She filled a glass with water and brought him a few pain reliever tablets.

"You don't have to wait on me," he said.

She stared him down. "Okay, what's with you? You obviously don't want me helping you. With anything. Why? What's the big deal?"

"I'm supposed to be protecting you."

"And you are."

He swallowed back the pills and stared at the dog.

"Look," she said. "People have been taking care of me my whole life. Now it's my turn. That's why I do the mission work, volunteer at church and run the tea shop. It's my way of returning the favor. I like doing it. I'd like to take care of you."

"No. Thank you."

"Why not?"

He snapped his gaze to meet hers. "I'm just not comfortable with it, okay?"

"Tough marshmallows." She went to the stove.

She wasn't going to give up and he wasn't sure how much fight he had left. He couldn't remember anyone ever taking care of him. Well, maybe Mom, before she got sick and their lives fell apart. But somewhere, deep down, he knew he didn't deserve someone's compassion, someone's love, and that was what caring for someone was about, right?

Krista's wall phone rang. "This can't go on all night or I'll go bonkers." She picked up the receiver.

"Hello…yes?"

She turned her back to Luke and he suspected it was Alan.

"I know…okay. I can't tonight. No, it's really not necessary. I understand but… Okay. Bye."

She sighed and hung up the phone.

"Bad news?"

She turned to him. "Alan. He wants to check in on me. I tried talking him out of it."

"No problem, I'll go back in the garage." Luke started to get up.

"You will do no such thing." She adjusted his arm around her shoulder to help him stand. "But you should probably sit in a chair instead of on my floor."

"I was getting used to your floor."

"Ha, ha." She pulled out a second chair and lifted his ankle, putting the ice pack on it. "Good, stay."

"Arf."

"See, how do you do that?"

"What?"

"One minute you're incorrigible and mean, and the next, you're joking around."

"I'm…" he paused. "Mean?"

"Sometimes, yeah." She planted her hands to her hips.

He glanced at his ice pack. She'd been good to him even though he'd ripped through her life like a lightning storm, blasting everything apart. "Sorry."

That was the second time he'd said that word tonight. Not like him. Not one bit.

Her wall phone rang again. "Oh, drat." She grabbed it. "Hello," she snapped. "Oh, hey, Nat. I thought you were…oh, no, I'm sorry. Hang on." Krista put her hand over the mouthpiece. "Can you give me a ride to and from work tomorrow?"

"Sure."

She turned back to her friend. "No problem, but it's at the shop, so you'll have to… I'm at home. No, I had to cancel, but I have a feeling he's coming over anyway…. Because I have to make sure Luke is okay."

"Luke can take care of himself," he called out.

She flashed her hand like a stop sign to silence him. It was a small, cute hand, one he realized he'd probably crush if he tried to hold it.

Still, he'd like to try.

He rolled his neck. Man, he needed a good work-out, something to get his balance back. Being around this woman made him go to strange places in his head, places he most certainly didn't belong.

"Sure, come over," she said to her friend. "Very funny. I'll see you later." She hung up and went back to the stove.

"More company?" Luke asked.

"Nat's Volvo died and she's supposed to meet Timothy in Muskegon for a romantic dinner, so she asked to borrow my car."

"And of course, you said yes."

"That's what friends are for." She opened a box of pasta and dropped it into the boiling water.

Friends. A foreign concept.

The slamming of a car door echoed from outside.

"Speaking of friends, that must be your boyfriend," Luke said.

"Could you watch the pasta?"

"Aren't you going to invite him in for dinner?"

"Probably not a good idea."

"Ah, he's the jealous type, I forgot."

She slipped errant strands of blond hair behind her ears, put on her jacket and hesitated. "If he does come in, you'll behave, right?"

Luke placed an open palm to his chest. "Like a true gentleman."

She shot him a half smile and went to greet Alan.

Luke got up to stir the pasta. He wasn't in the mood to verbally spar with Alan. Luke couldn't trust his edgy mood not to get him into trouble and pick a fight with the guy, who was most definitely not good enough for Krista Yates.

And Luke was?

He ripped his cell phone off his belt and called in, needing to remind himself why he was here in Krista's home.

"Agent Marks."

"It's Luke. Any word on the guys in Chicago or the blog site access?"

"The tech guy is still working on the source, but he says it looks like the hacker pretty much wiped everything clean."

"From a religious blog? That makes no sense."

"Unless she posted something she didn't realize was threatening. Oh, we traced her luggage. They put it on a truck this morning."

"And it's not here yet."

"They had other stops."

"That's too simple."

"At least you don't have to worry about Garcia's men. They're still in Chicago. Any flags in the community file you want us to follow up on?" Marks said.

"Actually," Luke paused. "I need a background check on Alan Jameson, loan officer at National Bank and Trust in Wentworth."

"Got it."

"Also, Phillip Barton and Lucy and Ralph Grimes."

"I'll get back to you."

"Thanks." The water boiled over, making a hissing

sound as it hit the burner. Luke turned down the heat. "I'll check in tomorrow."

Luke pocketed his phone and stirred the pasta with a fork, feeling better about helping out with dinner as opposed to her waiting on him. He glanced out the window, but Krista and Alan were nowhere in sight. He put down the fork and looked out the side window. They weren't there either.

Hobbling to the back door, he whipped it open.

No Krista. No Alan.

"Krista!"

TEN

Luke grabbed the crutches and went outside, his heart pounding against his rib cage. What kind of idiot would assume their visitor was the boyfriend? Luke, that's who, because he'd been so distracted by Krista's charming smile and gentle nature.

Practically falling off her porch, he stumbled out to the garage. Also empty. He stepped into the yard.

Calmed his breathing.

Scanned the property.

Listened for sounds of distress.

The haunting quiet of a snowy night rang in his ears. He ignored the chill in his bones and started up the driveway to the front of the house. He was greeted by blinding headlights.

Natalie got out of a taxi and looked at him in question. "What's wrong?"

"Krista," he panted, having crutch-sprinted up the driveway. "She's gone."

"Gone, where?"

"I have no idea."

Natalie casually adjusted her purse over her shoulder. "She's a big girl. I'm sure she'll be back soon."

He glared at Natalie and headed back to the house. Needed to call the chief. Find her.

Save her.

"Hey, don't you think you're overreacting?" Natalie said, following him.

He ignored her, couldn't get past the fact he'd failed again, let down an innocent.

Let down Krista.

"Luke, calm down," she said.

He spun on her. "You have no idea what's going on here."

"I'm her best friend, so you'd better tell me what on earth is going on."

He waved his hand in dismissal and pulled out his cell to call the chief.

"Who are you calling?"

"Chief Cunningham."

"Stop. Did you try calling her first?"

"No."

"That seems like an obvious thing to do, doesn't it?"

He clenched his jaw, unable to answer her. He wasn't thinking straight, couldn't even see clearly past the panic burning its way up his chest.

"Maybe there's a simple explanation." She dug out her cell phone from her purse and pressed Krista's speed dial. "Krista, thank goodness you answered." Natalie raised a brow at Luke.

Relief calmed his racing heartbeat. Then anger took hold. Krista left him, knowing it would make him insane with worry? Where could she have possibly gone and with whom?

"I'm at the house, where are you?... Uh-huh. Okay, yeah, well Luke is a little crazed, so as the saying goes, you should have called." Natalie chuckled. "Okay, I'll tell him."

Natalie dropped her phone in her purse. "She's with Alan. They're taking a walk around the block."

"It's too dangerous," Luke ground out.

"Hang on, what is so dangerous about a walk around the block?"

He went back inside, still reeling from panic. Natalie followed and dropped her coat on a kitchen chair. Roscoe ran up to greet her.

"A dog? What is going on?"

Luke ignored her and called the chief.

"Cunningham," the chief answered.

"It's Luke. Sorry to bother you, but Krista went out for a walk and I'm not sure it's safe."

"Alone? What's she thinking?"

"She's with Alan."

"Was probably his idea. I'll send a patrol to her neighborhood."

"Thanks."

"You bet."

Luke went back to stirring the pasta.

"Okay, enough of this cloak-and-dagger stuff," Natalie said. "What's really going on?"

Luke considered how much he should tell her, if anything.

"Look, buster." She grabbed the fork from his hand. "Since you've come to town all kinds of freaky stuff's been happening—the guy in her garage, the tea shop break-in. We're starting to think you're trouble. Yet the chief's on your speed dial. So what gives?"

"I'm here to protect Krista."

He thought maybe if Natalie knew how dangerous this situation was she'd help keep an eye on Krista, maybe she could work with him instead of against him. Still, he wouldn't share everything, especially not the fact they suspected a local of being a drug contact.

"I'm a federal agent," he said. "We think Krista has been targeted by a drug cartel."

"What?" She stepped back. "Our sweet Krista? Why?"

"Not sure." He stared her down. "Natalie, it's imperative that you not tell anyone about this. We need to keep it quiet in order to investigate properly. Can you do that?"

She nodded.

"Say yes," he said.

"Yes, of course."

"Even your fiancé," he pressed.

"Okay, sure. I'm just…stunned."

"So you can see why I'm worried about her."

"Why didn't she tell me?" she said.

"We asked her not to."

"But she'd never have anything to do with drugs."

"We think it's related to her mission trip. We're not sure how. But you're right, since her return from Mexico strange things have been happening and there's a possibility it's related to drug smuggling."

"I...I don't know what to say."

They shared a worried silence. If this woman truly cared about her friend, she'd do the right thing and be more protective. And not tell anyone about the threat.

"That's why you're here, isn't it?" she asked.

"Yes."

"And why you're sticking so close to her?"

"Yes."

Too bad it wasn't for other, nonprofessional reasons. *Yeah, buddy, that kind of thinking could get her killed.*

"But obviously I didn't stick close enough since she slipped out so easily. If it were up to me she'd stay in her house under armed guard."

"Don't even joke about it. She recoils from the thought of overprotective men, women or dogs, for that matter." With a smile, she stroked Roscoe's neck.

The thump of footsteps pounded up the back porch. The door swung open and Krista walked in, followed by Officer West, but no Alan. Good.

"Krista," Natalie said, rushing to her friend and hugging her. "Are you okay?"

"Hey, what's this all about?" Krista asked her friend.

"I was so worried," Natalie said.

"I'm fine, although a little peeved that you called the cops on me," she shot at Luke.

"You disappeared without an explanation." It was everything he could do not to lose his temper in front of these three women.

"Alan wanted some privacy. We needed to talk."

"You know it's not safe," Luke warned.

Krista glanced at her friend. "Another overprotective guy, just my luck."

"He told me what's going on," Natalie said.

Officer West shut the door. "And the chief fully briefed me as well."

"I'm fine," Krista huffed, taking off her coat. "Everyone's overreacting."

"I disagree," Luke said.

"I'd have to agree with Luke," Officer West said.

Krista squared off at Luke. "I needed to have a private talk with Alan, not within earshot of the kitchen."

"Did you get everything resolved?" Luke asked.

Krista shook her head and sat at the kitchen table.

"Krista?" Natalie said. "How did he take it?"

"I don't want to talk about it, especially not with an audience."

"Come on." With an arm around Krista, Natalie led her into the living room.

"Don't leave the house," Luke called after them. He couldn't stop himself.

A few minutes passed, Luke struggling with the raw panic that had probably shaved a few years off his life.

"That was a little over the top, telling her not to leave the house," Officer West said, leaning against the counter.

"I don't know what else to do. I'm with her and she disappears. The woman has no sense."

"She was trying to be sensitive to Alan's feelings. You can't fault her for that."

"I do if it puts her in danger."

"She's not like us. She's trusting and optimistic."

"And we are…?"

"Suspicious and cynical." She smiled. "Look, if it would make you feel better I could offer to spend the night on her couch until you find the perp."

"She'll probably fight us."

"It's worth a try. What's your next step with the case?"

"Investigating the locals."

"You really think someone in Wentworth is involved?"

"Absolutely. That's why I don't trust anyone, not even harmless Alan."

"Yeah, well that guy creeps me out so you're not alone there."

"You got any ideas how I can control this woman?" He nodded toward the living room.

"First, don't think in terms of controlling her. And second, let her know you trust her."

An impossible request.

The next morning Krista woke up feeling bad, both about making Natalie late for her dinner with Timothy, and the disastrous conversation with Alan. She'd nearly had him convinced to move on, explaining that she wasn't ready for a long-term relationship.

Then Officer West pulled up, police lights flashing. Horrified, Alan had left in a huff, feeling humiliated, which is what Krista had been trying to avoid.

"I can't believe Luke called the cops on me," she said to Anastasia. The cat peered down from the top of Krista's oak bureau. She'd meowed at Krista on and off all night, letting her owner know how displeased she was with their canine visitor.

Krista finished dressing and read a Bible passage about patience. She'd need an extra dose of it to deal with Luke McIntyre. He didn't want her help and demanded she tell him every detail of her plans, yet she knew he didn't tell her everything. She suspected he'd been given information from his superiors about the case, but wouldn't share it with her.

She went downstairs to make coffee and toast. The couch, where Officer West had insisted she sleep, was empty and the blankets folded neatly.

Krista wanted to feel appreciation for her house-guest, not resentment, but she couldn't help feeling smothered.

"Shake it off," she said to herself.

She stepped into the kitchen to find Luke sitting at the table drinking coffee, Roscoe by his side.

"Shake what off?" he said, glancing up from a smattering of open files. Some days she couldn't even describe the color of his eyes other than brilliant.

"My crabby mood," she recovered. Had she been staring into his eyes too long?

"Didn't sleep well?" he asked.

"Anastasia kept me up complaining about Roscoe."

"She didn't even see him."

"But she knew he was here. Want toast?"

"Sure. I boiled water, too. For your tea."

"Thanks." When he did stuff like that it made it hard for her to be cross with him.

"We've gotta move fast this morning," she said.

"Why's that?"

"The girls are opening for me, so I can cater a ladies' tea at the resort. We'll stop by the shop to pick up supplies, then head to Michigan Shores."

"A ladies' tea," he muttered.

"You can always stay back and work."

He closed a file folder and shot her a look like she'd just suggested he dress as Santa and greet little kids in the town square.

Twenty minutes later they swung by the shop. Luke was a big help, loading the boxes of scones, china cups and silverware into the trunk of his car. He wasn't using his crutches today, so his ankle must have felt better. Either that or he was covering his pain well.

Krista drove because she knew how to get there, and she suspected Luke wasn't fond of taking direction. She caught herself. Why did she think she knew so much about him, a virtual stranger?

As they headed to Michigan Shores Luke got a call and his congenial mood faded.

"I understand," he said. "Yes, I will." He pocketed his phone.

"Bad news?" she said.

He glanced in the side-view mirror and frowned. "Your luggage was supposed to be delivered yesterday. The truck driver claims he delivered it late last night."

"But we were home all night."

We were home all night. It sounded like they were a couple enjoying a night at home by the fire, watching a Hallmark movie.

"I guess we have to assume it's gone for good," he said.

"That's going to cost me. I'll have to buy a new wardrobe."

"Maybe the airline will reimburse you."

"Perhaps."

What really bothered Krista was the thought of someone, a stranger, going through her things, taking her comfortable jeans and her favorite wool sweater Mom had given her for Christmas before she'd moved to Florida.

"Don't think about it," he said.

He must have read her mind.

"Does that work for you? Not thinking about it?" Krista asked.

He glanced across the car and smiled. "Most of the time."

"Well, I'm a little old to use the 'ignore it and it will go away' tack."

"Yeah, you're ancient," he teased, glancing at the side-view mirror again.

"See anything interesting?"

"Not really."

They turned onto the long drive of the resort. Small cabins lined the property, and at the end of the driveway was the mansion-like lodge that housed guests and offered dining and entertainment. She pulled up to the front door and he put his hand on her shoulder.

"Give me a few seconds to scan the property, okay?"

His blue eyes caught her in a way that made her fidget in her seat. She looked away. "Sure."

He got out and glanced across the property, its leafless trees and tennis court, and pool that was packed with tourists during the summer season. Today a layer of snow blanketed the plastic covering.

Luke poked his head into the car. "Okay, let's go."

Krista went inside and got a few of the staff members to help bring in the boxes. The tea party was being held in a small room off the dining room with a picturesque view of Lake Michigan. Each table featured a vibrant centerpiece of alstroemerias, roses and carnations. It reminded her of the flowers she'd received from Alan last night.

Drat. In all the excitement she didn't get a chance to appreciate them. Or Alan. Was she making the wrong decision by cooling off their relationship? Maybe she wasn't seeing something in him, appreciating all his fine qualities.

Yet Mom always said Krista would know when she met the man who'd be her partner in Christ's love. She'd feel it in her heart.

She felt nothing for Alan but regret. Regret at leading him on, regret she couldn't care more about him, and regret that he couldn't accept her decision.

"What's wrong?" Luke asked, as he placed a saucer and teacup on a table.

"What do you mean?" she glanced at him.

"Something's bothering you."

"Just tired." Which she was. Besides there was no reason to bare her heart to him. This was a professional partnership, not a personal one.

"Maybe you should call in reinforcements to help out today," he suggested.

"Now you're telling me my business?" she said.

"Boy, you are crabby."

"Sorry." That wasn't like her, but she hadn't been able to get grounded since she returned home from the mission trip.

Luke shot her a tender smile. "Hey, we'll get these guys and put them away, and your life will get back to normal. This won't last forever."

For a split second, she wondered what forever would look like with Luke McIntyre. His smile faded, his blue eyes darkening.

"I should brew the tea," she whispered.

"What do you want me to do?"

Kiss me.

As if he'd read her thoughts, he leaned forward and

did just that. He placed a sweet, warm kiss on her lips that took the chill out of her chest and cast aside the worry from her mind.

It was the first time she'd experienced a kiss like this, a kiss that reached far deeper than her lips.

He broke the kiss and grabbed on to the back of a chair for support. Did the kiss affect him as much as it did Krista?

"Ankle's weaker than I thought," he said, glancing down at the floor.

"Goodness, sit down." She pulled out a chair and held on to his arm as he sat. This time he didn't pull away. He also wouldn't look at her.

"Luke?" she whispered, searching his face.

Someone cleared his throat from the doorway and Krista looked up. Chief Cunningham started toward them.

"Chief?" she said. "Did my luggage turn up?"

"It's not about your luggage." He glanced at Luke, then back to Krista. "There was an accident last night. Your friend Natalie is in the hospital."

ELEVEN

As they went into the hospital, Luke realized he'd never felt this helpless.

There seemed to be no words to comfort Krista. And he'd tried, talked more to her in the thirty-minute car ride to the hospital than he had all week. Talking, questioning, trying to get her to open up, share some of her worry so she wouldn't let it bottle up inside and eat away at her.

He didn't stop his attempts until they reached the hospital. With an arm around her shoulder, he escorted Krista down the corridor to Natalie's room. Yet she didn't seem comforted by his touch.

She seemed stunned, defeated.

Of course she was. They'd been on guard for a threat from Garcia's men, but no one could see this coming, a random car accident.

In Krista's car.

What if it wasn't a random accident? It was Krista's car that had been forced off the road. Krista should have been behind the wheel.

He'd focus on that later, when he wasn't reassuring Krista, holding Krista.

They approached room 314 and Krista hesitated. She looked up at him with such fear in her eyes, fear of her friend's condition.

"Do you want me to go in with you?" he offered, yet he wasn't sure how he'd do it. It wasn't the injured friend that scared him, but Krista's reaction.

A nurse came out of the room.

"How's she doing?" Krista asked.

"Stable," the nurse offered. "She's got some lacerations, a broken wrist, but otherwise, she's a very lucky lady."

"Can I see her, just for a minute? It might brighten her spirits," Krista said.

"Only one of you."

Luke nodded. "I'll be right here."

With a sigh, Krista went into the room and closed the door behind her.

He automatically put his hand to the door, wishing he could be there for her to ease some of the burden. Instead, he was an outsider again, looking on as someone he cared about was gutted by emotional pain.

He cared about her. He couldn't deny it any longer.

He paced the hallway outside Natalie's room and let himself have it for allowing that kiss to happen at the resort. What was he thinking? He wasn't. He was acting on instinct, naturally leaning forward, making the connection that was sure to haunt him for the rest of his life.

"Get away from her room!" Natalie's fiancé, Timothy, shouted coming down the hall.

A nurse chased after Timothy. "Sir, please keep your voice down."

"Get out of here before I beat you senseless!" Timothy threatened.

"Call security!" the nurse ordered.

Timothy charged. Luke grabbed the guy's arm, swung it around his back and slammed him against the wall.

"Calm down," Luke said.

"It's your fault! You brought this here!" Timothy squirmed against Luke's hold.

"Take it easy. You don't want them to kick you out of the hospital."

"Don't tell me what I want."

"You want to see her, don't you?"

"Stupid question."

"Then behave like a sane human being."

Timothy stopped struggling and Luke released him. The guy turned around and rubbed his shoulder. "I know it's your fault. I know you're not what you pretend to be. I heard you threatened Brent with a gun."

A security guard sprinted up to them and Luke waved him off.

"They should be kicking you out of the hospital and locking you up," Timothy said.

Chief Cunningham approached the three of them. "Timothy, take it easy."

"I don't care if he is your friend, Chief. This guy shows up in town and all kinds of violent stuff starts happening." He narrowed his eyes at Luke. "It followed him here."

"Back off, son. You're upset," the chief said.

"You bet I'm upset. Natalie is…she's…" His voice caught in his throat.

"She's going to be okay." The chief put a firm hand on Timothy's shoulder. "Why don't you go see her?"

Timothy turned and went into the hospital room. The chief glanced at the security officer. "Thanks. I've got this."

With a nod, the guard left.

Luke took a calming breath, easing the tension in his shoulders from being in the defensive position. He didn't want to hurt Timothy. Luke understood why the guy was so upset, but he didn't want Timothy drawing unwanted attention to Luke, either.

"It's an emotional time when a loved one is hurt," Chief Cunningham said.

Luke pushed back the memory of Karl dying in front of him. "Yep. Tell me about the car accident."

"Sounds like a pickup was passing Natalie and clipped her, sending the car into a ditch. Maybe a DUI—"

"Or not." Luke eyed the chief. "It was Krista's car. Maybe someone thought Krista was behind the wheel."

"Let's not jump to conclusions until we talk to Natalie. She's been in and out of it all night."

"All night? And her fiancé just got here?"

"They had a hard time with identification. Natalie

was unconscious when they got to her, and her purse was missing from the scene."

"You mean someone hit her, then stopped to swipe her purse?"

That could have been Krista, unconscious and vulnerable behind the wheel of the car, waiting for someone to help and instead being stalked and having her purse stolen.

Luke fisted his hand. "Then this was not a random hit and run."

Resting his hand on his firearm, the chief didn't argue. "Maybe Krista should take a vacation, leave town."

A pit grew in Luke's stomach at the thought of sending her away. But he knew better than anyone you could run from trouble, but that didn't mean you'd escape its reach.

"If they want her badly enough, they'll find her."

"What, then?"

"They stole Natalie's purse thinking it was Krista's. That's taking a big chance in public like that. We need to figure out what Krista's got that they want so badly."

"The luggage is still missing."

"Which means they got it, but didn't find what they were looking for. They thought she had it on her and sent someone to get it." Luke leaned against the wall and crossed his arms over his chest.

"She doesn't even know what they want," the chief said.

"Yeah, but by putting her in the hospital they gain access to her house."

"We should do a full search."

"I agree. And it wouldn't be a bad idea to have Officer West move in with Krista until this thing is over."

"I'll speak with her."

The door to Natalie's hospital room opened and Krista wandered out. She turned to Luke wearing a pale, distant expression.

"How is she?" the chief asked.

"Bruised. Tired. I offered to bring her some things from home but…" Her voice trailed off and she glanced over her shoulder at Natalie's room.

"But what?" Luke pushed.

"Timothy said he'd handle it."

"What else did Timothy say?" Luke asked.

She shook her head. "It's not important."

Maybe not, but it had upset her. Luke guessed the jerk must have been trash-talking him.

"I don't know if I should go or stay," she said, fiddling with her silver charm.

"We can hang around if you'd like," Luke said.

She shrugged. "Timothy made it pretty clear that he's got this covered. I guess we should head back."

The devastation in her voice caused an ache in Luke's chest. She felt so utterly helpless. He knew that feeling.

And he wanted to fix it, but hadn't a clue how.

"Krista, I'd like to search your house, if that's okay," the chief said.

"Sure. Whatever. I'm going to hit the ladies' room first." Krista nodded and walked down the hall.

"I'll get started on the search," the chief said. "You have any idea what we're looking for?"

"Wish I did."

"You'll be at the tea shop?"

"I'll be wherever she is."

Krista said silent prayers all the way back to Wentworth, prayers for Natalie's recovery and thanks to God that she wasn't injured more severely.

Krista simply couldn't imagine visiting her friend in worse condition than she'd seen her today. Bruises were forming around Natalie's eyes, her arms were scratched and her eyes bloodshot. She looked like she'd been beaten up.

Closing her eyes, Krista took a deep breath. *Please God, give me strength to help my friend, to know what to say to comfort her.*

Timothy had certainly said enough. He'd scolded Krista for bringing Luke with her to the hospital. Luke was the stranger who Timothy had decided was the cause of all the trouble in Wentworth over the past few days.

If only Timothy knew the truth. But he couldn't. No one could.

"She'll be okay," Luke offered, pulling into the parking lot of a family restaurant outside of Wentworth.

Again, it was like he'd read her thoughts.

"What are we doing here?" she asked.

"Lunch," he said.

"But—"

"Look." He parked and turned to her. "It's been a rough morning. Let's relax for a few minutes, have a cup of soup and regain some strength."

For once, Krista didn't mind being handled and told what to do. She didn't want to make any decisions or think for a little while. She just wanted to be.

They went inside Earl's Pancake House and took a booth in the corner. Luke ordered coffee and handed her a menu. She stared at the words, the block print swimming across the laminated beige page.

"Krista?" he said.

She glanced up and struggled to smile. "Sorry. I can't get the image of Natalie's bruised face out of my mind."

"I know." He reached over and placed his hand over hers. "She was actually very lucky."

"To think someone would bump into your car and drive off like that, without stopping to help or calling the paramedics." She sighed and welcomed the warmth coming from Luke's palm. "To think that could have been me."

He glanced down at their hands.

Reality struck her smack in the face. "Wait a second, do you think the accident was intentional? That some-one ran the car off the road thinking I was inside?"

Luke slipped his hand from hers and searched the restaurant. "Where's our waitress?"

She knew by his reaction that her suspicions were true. The collision was meant for Krista. It should be Krista lying in the hospital bed with bruises and bumps.

It should have been Krista who was almost killed, but instead it was Natalie.

And it was Krista's fault.

The buried pain of a five-year-old clawed its way up her chest, as flashes of memory assaulted her.

A tall man towering over her at the front door.

Krista telling him Dad was still at work.

Policemen standing on her front porch.

Mom collapsing when they told her...

Krista bolted from the booth and sprinted for the door. She needed fresh, cold air to shock her back to the present and snap the images from her mind.

"Krista!" Luke called after her.

She barely heard him. All she heard were her mother's cries and the policeman's questions. She remembered the look on her mother's face, a horrified look that haunted Krista to this day.

Krista thought it was the look of blame, because it was Krista's fault the bad man found her dad. In reality it was Mom's fear that the killer would come back to hurt Krista because she could identify him.

And then Krista and Mom ran. Just like Krista was doing right now.

Luke grabbed her arm. "Where are you going?"

Glancing around, she realized she'd made it into the parking lot, her instinct driving her to run, to escape.

Coward.

She'd never quite forgiven herself for uprooting Mom

from friends and her church community in California to hide out in Michigan with Gran.

"Krista, talk to me," Luke demanded.

She shook off the chill of a cold November day and looked into his blue eyes. "It's my fault. I should have been in the car instead of Natalie. Someone was after me, right?"

"We don't know that."

She pulled away from him. "It's true. Just like before."

"Before?"

"I can't go through that again, Luke. I won't let the people I love get hurt because of me."

"Listen, sweetheart." He cupped her shoulders with firm, gentle hands.

She wondered if he even knew he'd used the endearment.

"This is not your fault," he said.

It wasn't your fault, pumpkin. Mom's words. Krista never quite believed her. Just like she didn't believe Luke right now.

"Krista, do not blame yourself for this. You didn't put Natalie in the hospital."

"Sure I did. I loaned her my car."

"Because you're a good friend. Don't beat yourself up for that."

"You don't understand."

"Then come inside and explain it to me."

Krista glanced at the cars passing by. Her friend was nearly killed, but life went on as usual, just like it did when her father was killed. She never understood how life could go on as normal when her world had been blown apart.

With his forefinger to her chin, Luke guided her eyes to meet his. "Please, come inside."

When she looked into his concerned eyes, she felt grounded again. Her heart still raced, only not with anger at whoever rammed into Natalie. Her heart raced for a completely different reason.

With a comforting smile, he took her hand and led her into the restaurant. They went to their booth and hot coffee was waiting for them.

For once, she welcomed the bitter brew. She sipped the coffee and glanced out the window.

"I thought I'd left all that behind," she whispered.

"Your father?"

She nodded.

"Maybe you should take a break, a vacation."

She snapped her attention to him. "I won't run again."

"It's not running. It's…evading."

"I have a better idea. I'm going to help you catch them."

Luke leaned back in the booth. "Not a good idea."

"This whole time I've been taking things as they come, letting you and the chief figure out why these guys are in Wentworth. Well, no more. They've hurt my friend and I want to put an end to it."

"You're doing enough just by staying safe."

"I disagree. I could be doing more."

"I don't like the sound of this." He eyed his coffee.

"I'll find out whatever you need to know from the community. No one will suspect what I'm doing."

"I don't want you putting yourself at risk."

"I'm already at risk. You know that, Luke."

He crossed his arms over his chest. Worry lines creased his forehead and his lips pinched into a thin, contemplative line.

She thought he was worried about her, but then she noticed his gaze drift to the front of the restaurant.

He shifted out of the booth and planted his hand on her shoulder. "Stay here."

She turned around and watched him leave the restaurant, disappearing around the corner. Just then her cell phone rang. Hoping it was Natalie, she answered without looking at the caller ID.

"Hello, Nat?"

Nothing.

"Hello?"

"It should have been you in the car."

TWELVE

The black pickup cruising the parking lot fit the description of the one that rammed Natalie last night. It parked and someone opened the tinted window and blew cigarette smoke out the crack. Instinct drove Luke outside to investigate. Maybe he was being paranoid.

As Luke got closer, he slipped his hand inside his coat and gripped his firearm.

Suddenly the truck's engine roared and the driver spun out of the lot.

"Hey!" Luke called after him.

He was right. The driver of the car was keeping an eye on Krista. Had he been hovering close by when Krista fled into the parking lot a few minutes ago? The thought of the truck barreling toward her and finishing the job shot panic through Luke's veins.

One thing for sure: Garcia's men knew Krista wasn't lying helpless in a hospital bed. And she was still a target.

If only Luke knew what they wanted from her.

"Luke!" Krista called.

Luke spun around to see Krista racing toward him.

He scanned the trees surrounding the parking lot wondering if the driver of the pickup left someone behind to finish what they'd started last night.

She had to stop putting herself in danger like this.

"Someone called and—"

"I told you to stay inside." He grabbed her arm and pulled her back to the restaurant.

"What's wrong?" she asked, her eyes wide.

"Nothing."

She jerked her arm free. "Look, I can't help you or protect myself if you keep things from me."

But he wanted to; he wanted to distance her from the ugliness of the Garcia family. *Too late, buddy. You know that.*

"I think I just saw the truck that ran into Natalie," he said.

"Here? Why?"

When he hesitated, she said, "Oh, he was here for me. I guess he's the one who just called me, too."

"What did he say?"

"That it should have been me in the car."

Luke put his arm around her and led her inside. "I'm sorry."

With a shake of her head, she went back into the restaurant and sat down. The waitress approached them, order pad in hand. "You love birds staying this time?" she smiled.

Love birds. Right. Like that could ever happen between Krista and Luke.

"I'll have the soup and sandwich special, make it a burger," Luke said.

"And you, miss?" the waitress asked Krista.

"I'm not sure," she said, distracted as she eyed the menu.

"How about a grilled cheese sandwich and soup?" Luke offered.

Krista put down the menu. "Yes, I'll do that."

With a smile, the waitress took their menus and went into the kitchen.

"Krista," Luke said.

She glanced at him, but he sensed he didn't have her complete attention. Of course not, she was worried about what was coming next.

"I'm not going to let anything happen to you," he said.

"Thanks," she sighed and glanced out the window.

Now, if he could only keep that promise.

After stopping by Michigan Shores to pick up supplies, Krista insisted on going straight to the tea shop. A good thing in Luke's opinion because if she was at work, she couldn't go snooping around, looking for clues and getting herself hurt.

He appreciated her determination to help solve this case, but he didn't want her putting herself at risk. Yet he knew Krista. Once she set her mind on something, there was no changing it.

"It was lucky they had staff available to serve the ladies tea," she said.

He sensed guilt in her voice, guilt about having to abandon the tea party.

A few minutes later they pulled up to the tea shop and Krista opened her car door.

"Wait." He touched her arm.

"No, listen, they aren't going to kill me. If they do, they'll never find whatever it is they're looking for. I can't live in fear, Luke. I just won't do it." She whipped open her car door and headed for the shop.

Luke eyed her through the windshield, figuring this wasn't solely about the current threat, but that her past was adding fuel to her emotional fire. He couldn't imagine losing a father to murder and blaming yourself. Then again it was kind of like Luke blaming himself for his partner's death.

No, that was different. If Luke had been smarter, taken things slower, he would have sensed the danger instead of jumping in and putting himself and Karl at risk.

This case was messing with both his and Krista's heads in a big way. His priorities had shifted from finding the perp to protecting Krista. Yet they were one and the same, right?

Rationalize it any way you want. You're getting too involved with this case. With Krista.

He paced the cobblestone sidewalk next to the tea shop and called the chief.

"Cunningham."

"It's Luke. The truck that hit Natalie was stalking us, and Krista got a threatening phone call."

"Did you get a plate number on the truck?"

Luke gave him the number and leaned against the brick building. "Find anything at her house?"

"Not yet."

"Oh, and she's decided to launch her own investigation to expose the perp because they hurt her friend."

"Sounds like Krista."

Alan pulled up in his sedan and rushed into the shop. Didn't that guy get the message? Krista wasn't interested. End of story.

"They found Natalie's purse at a truck stop off Highway 31, money and credit cards still in the wallet."

"That's not what they were looking for."

"I'd give my bass fishing trophy to know what they wanted so badly."

"They broke into the shop looking for something. I'm going to do a little investigating around here, maybe find some answers."

"Good plan. We'll talk later."

"Thanks."

Luke pocketed his phone and headed for the back door, not looking forward to an Alan encounter.

When he entered the back, the place was up for grabs. Tori was frantically making sandwiches, while Krista had four teapots lined up, and was scooping loose tea into the strainers. The water in the sink was running, a timer was beeping and the phone was ringing.

And Alan hovered over Krista's shoulder. Luke wanted to grab the guy and toss him out the back door.

"When I heard about Natalie's accident in your car—"

"You're a great friend, Alan, but right now I need to focus on the lunch rush," Krista said. "I'm going to have to ask you to leave."

Even Luke was surprised by her short, businesslike tone.

Alan's expression changed from concern to anger. Krista couldn't see it. Her back was to him.

Luke took a step toward him. "Anything I can do, Krista?"

Alan snapped his head around to glare at Luke. The guy's squinty eyes radiated fire, and for a second Luke thought he could be more dangerous than he seemed.

"Finish filling the sanitizing sink, wipe down the counter and get Tori some clean dishes," she ordered.

"Excuse me," Luke said, shouldering his way past Alan into the tight quarters.

Although Luke ignored Alan and got to work, he sensed the guy hovering, waiting for something.

"As long as you're okay," Alan said to Krista.

"I'm fine, Alan. Thanks for stopping by."

A minute later the back door clicked shut. With a shake of her head, she set five timers to brew tea and shifted beside Luke to wash dishes. "I was rude, wasn't I?"

"Not rude. A little short maybe."

"I just couldn't help it. What with everything that's happened in the past twenty-four hours, I just couldn't deal with him."

"Understandable. Listen, the chief and Officer West are searching your house."

"For what?"

"Clues as to what you have that Garcia wants. Someone grabbed Natalie's purse after the crash, but when they found it the perp hadn't taken money or credit cards. You have any idea what they're after? Did you buy any trinkets or gifts that you brought back from Mexico?"

"Just a diary."

"Where is it?"

"In my suitcase."

"Krista, table four is complaining about their refill and table two says the soup is cold," Tatum said, hovering in the doorway holding a half-empty bowl of soup. "Oh, and I've gotta be at a thing in twenty minutes."

"What thing?" her sister questioned from the prep table.

"None of you business."

"Does Mom know about your thing?" Tori glared.

"Focus, girls," Krista said. "We're a team, remember?"

The girls stopped arguing and Luke admired her ability to shut them down.

"Luke, ladle a new bowl of soup, heat it in the micro for a minute and I'll take it out. Tatum, finish up the dishes. I'll take over the dining room. Tori?" Krista stepped into her line of vision. "Good job on the food prep. You comfortable here or do you want the dining room?"

"I'm good."

"Great, then let's move it."

* * *

After a few hours of serving customers the guilt and fear started to ease. Guilt about Natalie's accident and fear of being stalked and attacked. Krista was just too exhausted to worry.

She wasn't too tired to chat with customers, ask pleasant but pertinent questions and gather information for Luke's investigation. She listened for mention of anything odd or out of line with the normal happenings of Wentworth.

It was typical for her to talk up customers. She liked the interaction and liked hearing what they had to say about their families, current events and plans for vacations. Some customers even asked about Natalie.

That connection was the real joy of owning a shop like this, a connection she suspected Luke found useless, maybe even terrifying.

They locked up at five and headed home. She steeled herself against what her house would look like. Did the chief and Officer West rip the place apart? She hoped not but would accept it if it meant getting that much closer to ending this nightmare.

"You're quiet," Luke said, pulling into her driveway.

"Pensive."

"I saw you grilling your customers. You shouldn't do that."

She squared off at him. "I wasn't grilling anyone. I was being friendly."

"Still, someone could figure out you're playing investigator."

"Oh, yeah, because I got great clues today," she said with sarcasm in her voice. "Ruth and Gerry are going on a cruise in March, Nancy Patterson sold her vintage sewing machine, and the Cooper boys were suspended for two days for squirting hair gel on their biology teacher's keyboard."

"What would give a kid the idea to do that?" .

"They're bored. I suspect smart, too."

"That's all you got?" he joked.

"Annette Winters said they were looking forward to my cranberry scones at the church potluck tonight." She glanced at Luke. "I totally forgot about that one."

"Don't go. Tell them you've had a rough week, you're still jet-lagged and—"

"I can't renege on cranberry scones, no matter how tired I am." *Or what criminals are after me.*

Luke gripped the steering wheel tighter. He seemed genuinely worried about her, which meant he cared about her more than an agent would normally care about a witness, right? Or was he worried about being around church folk? Because wherever she went, he'd surely be inches behind her.

They parked on her driveway and could hear Roscoe barking from the garage. He was a good watchdog, for sure.

With files tucked under one arm, Luke escorted her to the back door with a gentle hand at her elbow.

She realized she liked having him close, enjoyed the

supportive hand of a strong man. Then she remembered that all too soon he'd be gone. She quickened her pace and pulled away from him.

She was starting to fall for the grumpy federal agent, against her will and all good sense in her head.

Once inside, she dropped her purse on the table and tentatively eyed the living room. It wasn't too bad. Sure, things were out of place, but it wasn't messy.

She was strung tight, like a tennis racket, and needed to decompress with a little baking, maybe blogging.

"I'm going to check on Roscoe, let him out," Luke said, coming up behind her. "You stay here, got it?"

"Where else would I go?"

"Off to do more snooping around? I don't know."

"I'm too exhausted to do anything but collapse."

"Good. I'll be back in a few minutes." He left and she shut and locked the back door.

Alone. Finally. She welcomed the solace without her shadow looking over her shoulder. Sure, she appreciated his help today at the shop, and of course she was thankful that he was here in Wentworth to protect her.

But she desperately needed time alone to breathe, think and fully come down from the adrenaline rush that started this morning when she visited Natalie.

Speaking of which, she hadn't spoken to Nat since she'd seen her at the hospital. Krista had called, but Timothy intercepted the call and said Nat was too tired to talk.

She pulled out ingredients for cranberry scones and

got busy, while dialing the hospital to check on her friend.

"Mercy General."

"Room 314, bed A please."

"One moment."

While Krista waited she assembled the dry ingredients. The line rang repeatedly, six, seven, eight times, but no one answered. She cut the butter into the dry mixture, added the cranberries and sugar in a separate bowl and beat together the cream and egg. A good thing she could make these in her sleep.

"Answer, already," she whispered.

"Mercy General."

"Oh, hi. I was trying to reach my friend, Natalie Brown?"

"Hold please."

Krista blended the dry mixture with the cream mixture and dumped the dough on the counter. Kneading the dough seemed to ease her nerves a bit.

The operator came back on the line. "Miss Brown was discharged late this afternoon."

"Really? She didn't look in any condition to leave the hospital."

"I'm sorry, ma'am, I can't give out information about a patient's condition. I can only tell you if she's here or not."

"Okay, thank you."

She spread and cut the dough into triangles, placed them on the cookie sheets and popped them into the oven.

Natalie, out of the hospital? Curious.

She set the timer for twenty minutes, washed her hands and called Nat's house. The call went to voice mail.

"Hey, Nat, it's Krista. Could you give me a call and let me know what I can do to help? Thanks."

Krista thought it odd that Nat was released and wasn't answering her home phone. Then again, Timothy was probably micromanaging her, protecting her from too much activity or stress.

Although Krista's feelings had been hurt by Timothy's harsh words earlier today, she knew they were born of love for his fiancée. The thought of her being seriously injured was tearing him apart.

Krista hoped someone would someday love her as much as Timothy loved Nat. Well, Alan had claimed he loved her.

"Move on," she whispered to herself.

But she couldn't really move on until this case was solved, she got her life back to normal and Luke disappeared, back to his work chasing criminals.

Criminals like the ones hounding her. They broke into her shop, her home and her blog. Well, they might be threatening her from the shadows, but they couldn't stop her from blogging. The blog was her way of taking control of her situation. She'd re-create it and bring joy to others' lives, regardless of the criminals threatening her.

She grabbed her purse and sat at the computer nook. Blogging about her mission trip always brightened her spirits. So someone breached her Faithgirl blog. She'd just start a new one using a different name.

She grabbed her key chain from her purse and pulled off the thumb drive. She stuck it into her computer and created a new blog on blogworld.com.

Scanning through her pictures helped her instantly relax as she remembered how it felt to help the children in the small village outside of Mexicali. Krista felt like she was part of something bigger than herself, something Christ had called her to do. All the petty stresses of life dissolved and the tightening in her chest over her current situation eased a bit.

Luke tapped on the back door. She got up and let him in. "What, isn't Roscoe coming?"

"I thought I'd better ask first."

"Sure, you can bring him in."

While Luke went back to the garage, Krista put up the baby gate between the kitchen and living room. "Sorry, Anastasia," she called into the house. The princess cat had been in hiding ever since Roscoe's appearance.

Just as Luke and Roscoe came up the back steps, someone rang the front doorbell.

"I'll answer it," Luke said. "You have your cell?"

She nodded and grabbed it out of her purse.

"Be ready to call for help. Stay out of sight, got it?"

"Sure."

A few seconds passed, her heart pounding, Roscoe dancing by the baby gate, wanting to get to Luke.

She heard him open the front door. Then nothing. It

was eerily quiet. A few seconds later the door shut, and she heard footsteps headed her way.

Were the footsteps even Luke's? Should she call the police? She whipped her head around and spotted a can of starch. She grabbed it and pointed at whoever was coming into the kitchen.

Luke stepped over the baby gate carrying her suitcase.

"They finally delivered it. Fantastic." She reached for the black suitcase, but Luke cautioned her.

"This is evidence."

"Luke, I really miss my sweater. Please?"

He placed the suitcase on the kitchen table, grabbed a paper napkin and unzipped it, slowly.

"Come on, come on," she joked.

"Look, we don't know who dropped this off. No one asked me to sign, it was just there on your porch."

"You're right. Sorry."

He finished unzipping it and flipped it open.

She spotted her sweater, all right, shredded to pieces, along with the rest of her clothes.

THIRTEEN

"Don't touch anything," Luke said, studying the suitcase. "I'll call the chief to come get this for forensic testing."

Luke closed the suitcase, wanting to shut out the violence that had destroyed Krista's things. He wanted to wipe that look off her face. Was it fear or sadness? Either way, it tore him apart.

"Was that really necessary?" she said. "The whole shredding my clothes thing?"

"I'm guessing they meant to frighten you." He eyed her. "Are you frightened?"

She leveled him with brilliant green eyes. "I'm angry."

"Good, then they failed." He glanced at the bag.

"I don't suppose the airline will reimburse me for my clothes?"

"It's possible. Why don't you call them and give it a try?"

"After I finish uploading pictures to my blog." She sat down at the computer.

"I thought—"

"I created another one." She shot him a victorious grin.

"Nice."

She went back to work on the blog. It amazed him how she was able to snap out of her anger and launch into a new project. But then in her mind, blogging about her mission trip was probably her way of taking control of the chaos.

He admired her for that. As he pulled out his phone to call the chief, he realized he admired a lot of things about Krista. Topping the list was the fact she did not let Garcia's men rattle her to the point of locking herself up in her house. On some level he wished she would. It would make his job a lot easier.

"Cunningham."

"Chief, it's Luke McIntyre. Krista's suitcase was anonymously delivered to the house. Everything inside was destroyed."

"Sorry to hear that. Want me to get it to the forensics lab in Grand Rapids?"

"That would be great." Luke moved the suitcase off the table and next to the door.

"I'll send an officer over."

"Thanks."

"You coming to the potluck tonight?" the chief asked.

"How'd you know?"

"Word travels fast in Wentworth. Like a sled goin' ninety down a luge track."

"I should have figured."

"How's Krista doing?"

"She's—" he paused and glanced at Krista, focused on the computer screen. "Determined."

"Good. I'll see you later, then."

"Yep." Luke turned to Krista and eyed the new blog over her shoulder. She dropped in a photograph of her kneeling and talking to a little girl.

"Nice shot."

"Thanks. That's Maria. Her brother, Armando, was injured by a drug dealer's bullet."

"Wait, so your mission work was that close to Garcia's compound?"

"I don't know. I guess it's possible."

Luke scooted a chair next to Krista and she turned to him. "What?"

"Maybe you saw something you weren't supposed to, or heard something or—"

"Like what?"

"I don't know." Luke glanced at the floor and back up at Krista. "Names, do you remember hearing any names, or places or anything about Michigan?"

She shook her head. "No, sorry. I would have remembered that."

The timer went off and she jumped up to pull out the scones. The kitchen smelled of home, not like a home Luke had ever known, but he imagined this is what a happy one smelled like.

"We'll head over to church in about an hour, after I whip up another two dozen," Krista said.

"They smell great."

She measured some flour and dumped it into a bowl. "Didn't your mom ever bake for you?"

"No." A one-syllable answer. He couldn't risk anything more.

"Huh. I thought all moms baked." She put cream and sugar into another bowl and blended it.

She glanced at him, expectant.

"My mother had—" he paused "—health problems."

Krista hesitated as she mixed the dry ingredients in with the creamy mixture. "I'm sorry."

"It's fine."

His way of shutting down. If he didn't, he might end up in that place where he blamed himself for her drinking, and the health complications that followed. It must have been difficult raising a kid like Luke all by herself.

"What?" Krista prodded.

Luke glanced up.

"You got a strange look on your face. Were you thinking about her?"

"No, I was trying to figure out how to keep from eating all your scones before we get to church."

"Very funny. Like I believe that."

"Believe it. They smell delicious."

Krista smiled and glanced over her shoulder at him. Her gaze caught on the suitcase by the door and her smile faded. He wanted to do something, brush his thumb across her cheek and make her smile again.

"What kinds of things do you need to know about people?" She snapped her attention back to kneading the dough.

"I'd rather you not—"

"I'm going to, so tell me what you're looking for."

"A large influx of money, someone bragging about buying expensive jewelry or a new car, when you know they probably couldn't afford it. Anyone who's taken a trip recently, people who vacation in Mexico."

"Anything else?"

"That's a good start."

With a spatula she transferred the scones to a cooling rack, put scone dough on the baking sheet and slid it into the oven.

"One more batch and we're ready to go. Wanna taste?"

"Sure."

She dropped two scones on a plate and put the kettle on.

"Must have tea with your scone," she said.

Her wall phone rang and she grabbed it. "Hello. Hello. I'm sorry, I can't hear you."

Luke stepped up beside her and leaned in to listen. Wasn't easy to stay focused with the heat of her skin warming his cheek.

"Who is this?"

Heavy breathing echoed across the line.

Luke took the phone from her. "There's a trace on this call."

More breathing. Luke hung up and sat down at the kitchen table. "Is the tea ready?"

"Almost." She sat down and studied him. "Do you think that was…?"

"Doesn't matter. They can't touch you as long as I'm here, but it wouldn't hurt to put a trace on your phone. I'll mention it to my supervisor when I call in."

"Thanks," she said.

"Don't expect much. If they're smart, they'll hang up before we can get a location."

"Well, thanks anyway." She continued to study him.

Luke patted his leg for Roscoe's attention. He didn't like it when Krista looked too deeply into his eyes. He feared she'd see things no one else could see, things Luke tried to hide even from himself.

"Might as well go through some files while we wait," he said, opening a folder. Work would distract him and keep him focused on what he was here to do, because he surely was not here to fall for a sweet, Christian woman with a generous spirit.

She deserved better.

"Can I help?" she said.

"Nah, thanks."

Resting her chin on an upturned palm, she didn't take her eyes off him.

"See anything interesting?" he said.

"Yeah, actually, I do."

He ignored her comment and the kettle whistled, saving him from another uncomfortable moment. Why?

It's not like she was judging him or criticizing him. That wasn't Krista's way. No, it seemed more like she was trying to figure him out, maybe even appreciate him.

Not possible.

She put a flowered teapot on the table, and a flowered plate with a scone in front of him. "They taste best when they're warm."

He closed his file and took a bite of the scone. It tasted like nothing he'd ever tried before, the tart cranberries complemented the sweetness of the flaky biscuit.

"You like?" She smiled.

"This is great."

"Good." She poured tea into two teacups and leaned back in her chair.

They slipped into a comfortable silence, enjoying tea, scones and each other's company. He shouldn't be this comfortable or this relaxed. Luke should be on guard, waiting for the next assault. He glanced at Roscoe, who was happily lying beside Luke's chair.

He scanned the kitchen and his gaze caught on the photograph of Krista, her mom and grandmother. Somehow he felt the closeness and intimacy of a loving family.

Roscoe growled low in his throat, snapping Luke out of the moment.

"What is it, boy?" Luke rubbed his neck.

Roscoe whined, then barked and rushed the kitchen window. Luke flipped off the light to get a better view. He stepped closer to the window and spotted a squad car pulling into the driveway.

"Luke?" Krista said with worry in her voice.

"It's the officer for the suitcase. I'll take it out to him."

"Great, I'll go get ready."

Luke grabbed the suitcase, opened the door and met the cop on the back porch.

"How about some I.D.?" Luke asked.

The kid flashed his badge. It read John Fritz, Community Service Officer. Luke handed him the suitcase. "You don't carry a firearm?"

"Not as a community service officer."

"Okay, well, be careful with this."

"Yes, sir."

Luke watched the CSO put the suitcase into the back of his squad car and take off.

Luke went into the kitchen and paused. He realized Roscoe could have been barking at one of Garcia's men stalking the house instead of the service officer pulling into the drive. And Luke had been so comfortable, so relaxed, that he hadn't even realized he'd drifted off into fantasyland.

"Don't let it happen again," he warned himself.

He couldn't breathe.

Luke grabbed at his shirt collar, but realized he'd already unbuttoned it. The community room at Peace Church was packed. Packed with conversation, love and laughter.

And he couldn't take much more.

"Here," Krista said, shoving a plate full of food at him. "You look pale."

"That obvious?"

"Only to me." She glanced across the room. "I love these events."

"That makes one of us." He couldn't stand how all these people got into each other's business and offered advice, butted into someone's life without being asked.

"What freaks you out so much?" she asked.

"I'm not good with people."

She smiled up at him. "You're good with me."

He opened his mouth to quip back, but couldn't come up with the right words.

She was right. He didn't have to work at being comfortable with Krista, even though she scared him, especially her ability to see through his angry exterior into the heart of a little boy.

A wounded little boy.

"I don't like that look," she said. "Have a cookie."

She grabbed a sugar cookie off his plate and held it to his mouth.

"Well, ain't that sweet?" Chief Cunningham said walking up to them.

Krista placed the cookie back on the plate and brushed off her fingertips. "Just trying to cheer up our friend with some sugar. You two talk while I make the rounds."

"Haven't you already made the rounds?" Luke said, desperate to get out of here.

"Can't hurt to make them again." With a smile she breezed into the crowd, touching a young woman's elbow to join in on a conversation.

"How you holding up, son?" the chief asked.

"Do I look that bad?"

"No, not bad at all. Just uncomfortable."

"I'm not used to these kinds of things."

"Guessed as much." The chief glanced across the room. "Anyone from the files look like a person of interest?"

"Phillip Barton has relatives in Mexico. Is he here?"

"Over by the punch bowl. Probably spiking it, if I know Phillip."

Phillip was mid-fifties with short, black hair and a square jaw.

"Tell me about his business," Luke asked.

"Said he owns a seat on the board of trade and doesn't need to work. Moved to Wentworth five years ago and opened a boat cruise business for tourists. Takes them out on Silver Lake and Lake Michigan. Does pretty good, I think."

"He fits the profile."

Luke spotted Alan hovering behind Krista.

"Alan the banker is a possible," Luke said.

"You think he's smart enough to be connected to a drug cartel?"

"We're not looking for smart. We're looking for someone who can take orders," Luke said.

"Did you finish going over the mission group list?"

"I did. All twelve seem clean to me. I'm starting to think Garcia's men might have smuggled something into the country through someone's luggage without their knowledge."

"And it was to be collected by their man in town?"

"Makes the most sense."

"Which doesn't explain why they're after Krista."

"No, it doesn't."

Which is what kept Luke from getting a good night's sleep. He not only had to figure out how Garcia's men got drugs into the country and where the drugs ended up, but also why they were after Krista. Until he knew why, she wouldn't be safe.

An elderly woman with silver hair and a warm smile wandered up to the chief and Luke with a pan in one hand and spatula in the other. "Boys, did you try my blueberry streusel?"

"Not yet, ma'am." Luke nodded to his plate. "I'd better finish my dinner first."

"Nonsense." She cut a small wedge and placed it on top of Luke's other desserts. "So, how are things at the tea shop?"

"Ma'am?" Luke questioned.

"You're the handyman, correct? How're the projects coming along?"

"Good, very good."

"I'm so glad. I don't know what we'd do without Grace's Tea Shop. It's magical, you know." She smiled.

"Yes, ma'am."

A younger woman in her thirties approached Luke. "Hi, I'm Julie Sass. My daughters work for Krista."

Luke shook her hand. "Luke McIntyre."

"The girls say you've been doing wonders at the shop." She leaned closer. "And with Krista." She winked.

Luke shot a panicked look at the chief, who shrugged.

"Ah, well, I'm pretty good with drains, but nearly killed myself hanging Christmas lights," Luke said, avoiding the comment about Krista.

"I heard. How's the ankle?"

"It's good, thanks."

"Mr. McIntyre?" An elderly woman stepped in front of the streusel lady. "I'm Delores Frupp, Doe for short. If you have any pain from the ankle, I use arnica, an herbal cream that reduces the swelling."

"Thanks, I'll remember that, but I'm really—"

"Or aloe vera. That's always helped me," streusel lady offered.

"R.I.C.E.," Julie Sass said. They all looked at her.

"Rest, ice, compression and elevation. That's what the coach told Tori to do when she sprained her ankle in soccer."

The three women discussed the benefits of the various forms of first aid for sprained ankles. Luke glanced at his plate of food, wondering why it bothered him that they seemed to care so much about him.

It reminded him of something, someone…

The many someone's from his childhood church.

They'd visit once a month after services bringing food and clothes, sometimes toys for Luke.

He'd hear the doorbell ring and he'd hide in his room as Mom welcomed the group into the living room, offering them a beverage…

While she threw back her fourth glass of scotch.

At one in the afternoon.

Buried memories shot to the surface, blinding him, suffocating him.

The women's voices, the cacophony of the crowd rose to an unbearable pitch. His heart pounded against his chest.

"I gotta go." He handed the chief his plate and made for the door.

He needed fresh air, needed to get out of here and shake the memories from his mind. Get his head back in the game.

Mom was an alcoholic.

He'd never admitted it before.

Shame coursed through him.

He stormed out the back of the church toward the garden.

That's why she died: because she drank herself to death. Everyone in town, all the church people knew it.

They knew his shame.

Which was why, after two years in foster care, he'd lied about his age and joined the army.

He ran, just like he was now. Had to get away from the crowd of people inside who reminded him of his childhood church community, the people who knew the truth—Luke was so bad that he drove his mother to kill herself with booze.

He went outside to the back garden that was covered in snow, the plants dormant until spring.

Dormant, like his memories.

Until now.

"Mom," he whispered as frustration ripped through his chest.

A crunching sound drew his attention and he turned.

Just as something hit him in the back of the head. He dropped to the ground, face-first into the snow. His cheek chilled as he struggled to focus, to figure out...

He gasped and passed out.

FOURTEEN

When Krista saw Luke bolt out of the community room, she wondered if he'd received word about the case. Then she caught the look in his eye and she instantly wanted to follow him, find out what caused the desperation she read there.

It wasn't about the case. It ran deeper than that and she wanted to help him.

Unfortunately she was surrounded by church friends who wanted to hear more details about the mission trip. She directed them to her new blog site, and politely excused herself, saying she had to visit the ladies' room.

She made a beeline for the back door, whipped it open and froze at the sight of a tall, hooded figure standing over a motionless body in the snow.

Even from here she recognized the fallen man's black boots. Luke's boots.

"Luke!" she cried.

The hooded man sprinted away, disappearing through nearby bushes.

She opened the door to the community room and

grabbed Tori Sass, who happened to be standing there with her boyfriend. "Tori, go get the chief and send him out back, now."

Krista turned and rushed down the back steps, instinct driving her across the property. Luke's normally strong, large body looked dwarfed in the snow.

Panic flooded her chest at the thought of him being—

"Krista?" the chief called from the back door.

"It's Luke, someone hurt him!" She skidded to a stop and kneeled beside him, brushing her hand against his cheek. He was so cold, so still.

The chief rushed up behind her.

"Did you see—"

"The bushes." She pointed, but could hardly say more in her distraught state.

The chief called across the property, but she could hardly hear him past the pounding of her heart.

"Luke, open your eyes," she whispered, placing her palm to his cheek to warm him.

Please God, don't take him yet. Not like this.

"What happened?" Dr. Langston said, rushing up to her. A small group was forming.

She glanced up at the tall, elderly doctor. "I'm not sure. He's unconscious."

"Krista?" Luke moaned.

She turned to him. "Luke, you're okay, it's going to be okay." She glanced at the doctor, looking for confirmation.

He motioned for her to move aside and she did, but she didn't break the contact with Luke's cheek.

"Do you remember what happened to you, son?" Dr. Langston asked.

"No, sir."

"I need to call an ambulance," Krista said.

"No." Luke grunted and pushed up with his hands. Krista helped him stand.

He wavered a bit and she put her arm around his waist to steady him. Dr. Langston came around the other side for support.

"Let's get him into the pastor's office," the doctor said.

Krista nodded and the three of them shuffled past the growing crowd into the back of the church.

"Give us space," the doctor ordered the group, then nodded at Julie Sass. "Can you get my car keys out of my parka inside and get my bag out of the car?"

"Absolutely." She ran ahead, while Krista and the doctor helped Luke up the back steps and down the hallway toward Pastor White's office.

The concerned mumblings of church friends echoed down the hall behind them. There was no way around it, everyone was going to find out who Luke was and why he was here.

And how much danger Krista had somehow brought back with her to Wentworth.

"What happened?" Tatum asked someone behind them.

"Looks like he slipped on the ice. Happens to the

best of us," the chief offered. "Everyone, back to the potluck."

Krista understood his motivation to keep the real danger a secret. His job was to protect the people of Wentworth, and find the Garcia threat as quickly and quietly as possible.

Krista and the doctor led Luke around the corner to a chair in the pastor's office. She kneeled beside him. She didn't like the way he looked. His skin was pale and his eyes creased with confusion.

"Do you feel faint?" the doctor asked.

"No, but I've got a massive headache."

Julie rushed into the room. "Your bag."

Dr. Langston opened it and pulled out a penlight to examine Luke's eyes.

"Let's start with a few questions," the doctor said, shining the light in one eye, then the other. "What day of the week is it?"

"Friday."

"What's your name?"

"Luke McIntyre."

"Where are you?"

Luke glanced around the room. Krista mouthed "church" and Doc Langston raised a brow.

"Sorry, sorry," Krista said. She couldn't help herself. She wanted him to be okay.

Julie touched Krista's arm. "Come here," Julie motioned.

Krista glanced at Luke and he shot her a hint of

a smile, indicating he'd be okay without her hovering over him.

She wandered to the other side of the room with Julie. "What happened?" Julie asked.

"I have no idea. I went looking for Luke, and spotted some guy standing over him in the snow."

"What happened to the guy?"

"When I called out for Luke, he took off."

Julie's gaze drifted to the doctor's examination of Luke. "So some guy attacked Luke?"

"Let's not assume that. But he sure didn't do anything to get help."

The chief came into the pastor's office. "Well, that's more excitement than we've had at a potluck in ten years. They need you out there, Julie. Something about the kids spiking the punch?"

"Oh, no." Julie rushed out of the office and the chief closed the door.

"How is he?" the chief asked.

"Fine," Luke said.

"His eyes look fine, motor skills good," Doc Langston said. "He's got a nasty contusion on the back of his head. You get that from falling on the ice, son?"

"I…" He paused. "Don't remember, sorry."

"Nothing to be sorry about." The doctor stood and glanced at Krista. "Wouldn't hurt to put ice on his head, get fluids into him and ask him questions every hour or so until he goes to bed. If he seems disoriented or starts vomiting, get him to the clinic."

"Should I take him to the clinic now?" Krista said.

"No," Luke argued. "Just get me some aspirin and I'll be fine."

The doctor glanced at Luke, then Krista. "I don't think it's serious. Still, wish you could remember what happened, son."

Luke rubbed the back of his head. "Me, too."

"Well, I'm headed back inside." Dr. Langston packed up his bag.

"Thanks." The chief opened the door, and closed it behind him.

Luke glanced up at Krista. "Stop looking at me like that."

"Like what?"

"Like I'm dying or something."

"I was worried."

"Don't be. I've been through worse."

The comment stung, especially because it drove home the violence he'd survived as a federal agent, violence that disturbed her way too much to be a part of her life.

"What happened out there?" the chief asked.

"I told you, I don't remember," Luke snapped.

"Luke," Krista hushed.

"I'm frustrated, okay? One minute I'm in the community room staring at a plate of food, and the next thing I know I'm facedown in the snow."

"Do you remember handing me your plate and saying you had to get outside?" the chief said.

Luke's eyebrows furrowed and dawning colored his blue eyes, then he glanced away. "No."

Either he didn't remember or he didn't want to share. Krista guessed it was door number two.

Krista wondered if his disorientation was freaking him out. She touched his shoulder. "It's okay. You're safe."

He stood and paced to the window, breaking their connection.

She wasn't sure how much more of this she could take. Although his reaction was probably born of frustration and helplessness, it cut deep into her heart.

"I need to talk to the chief." Luke turned to her. "Alone."

"I thought we agreed you'd keep me in the loop from now on?"

"Just…" He bit back what he was about to say. "Can you get me some aspirin?"

"Sure." Krista left before doing something stupid, like getting in his face and demanding he stop shutting her out.

She headed down the hall, calming her breathing, fighting back the wave of frustration that made her tear up.

Why did he get to her like this?

Because you care about him more than you're supposed to. Her heart plummeted when she saw his body lying there in the snow. If he had died…

No, she couldn't think about that now.

Thank you, Lord, for protecting Luke. Please help me with my feelings for him, and please help me show him the grace of God.

* * *

He was angry and embarrassed, and the pain reliever did little to ease the pounding in his head. And all he wanted to do was go back to his temporary home and chill out with Roscoe.

But Krista was determined to check in on Natalie and bring her food from the potluck. Krista was concerned because she hadn't spoken to her friend since she'd been released from the hospital.

"Head still hurt?" she asked.

"Yep."

"Want me to drop you at home?"

"Nope."

"I'm sure I'd be safe at Natalie's."

"Just as I was sure I'd be safe at church." The minute he said it he regretted the words. They weren't necessary. He didn't have to bite her head off.

"Sorry," he said.

"I know."

He suspected she really did know, and that terrified him. He could face off some of the deadliest criminals, but what scared him more was this woman's ability to see into his heart.

"I'll only be a few minutes," she said, turning down a side street.

"I'm going in with you."

"I'm not sure Timothy will like that."

"He'll get used to me." He eyed her. "You have."

She smiled, then redirected her attention to the street. A good thing.

"That's odd," she said.

"What?"

"Her house is completely dark."

"Maybe she's asleep."

"No, she always leaves the porch light on, and the light in the living room is on a timer. It stays on all night for her cat."

"Cat's afraid of the dark, is it?"

"Natalie thinks so."

"Drive past the house a block and park."

"But—"

"Please, just do it."

With a disgruntled sigh, Krista passed Natalie's house and pulled up behind a blue sedan.

"Call her," Luke ordered.

Krista dug in her pocket for her cell and made the call.

"Voice mail," she said.

"Try again."

She called her friend, tapping her fingers on the steering wheel. "It's no use, she's not—" Krista sat up straight. "Natalie?… Where are you?… But… I know, but…"

While Krista caught up with her friend Luke scanned the neighborhood. He was seeing shadows everywhere now, behind trees, beside cars, even in living room windows.

He'd let his guard down earlier, allowed ghosts of the past to mess with his head and throw him off course for only a few minutes. That's all it took for someone to whack him but good.

But why? If they'd wanted him dead they would have finished him off in the church garden.

Then again, it seemed like Krista had interrupted the attack. He fisted his hand. She could have been kidnapped, or worse, and he would have been lying there, unconscious. Helpless. Unable to protect her.

"I don't understand," Krista said. Luke figured she was still talking to her friend. "Luke?"

He turned to her perplexed expression. "Excuse me?"

"She's at Timothy's. I guess he doesn't want her at home by herself."

"That's decent of him."

"He's really not the nurturing type and has little patience."

"He must love her."

The words hung in the air between them. Love, a confusing and complicated emotion at best.

"She's lucky," Krista whispered, and started the car.

"So we're going to Timothy's?" Luke asked.

"No. She doesn't want to upset him and he, well, doesn't want me around right now."

"What's that about?"

"He blames me for the car accident."

"That's ridiculous."

"He feels the way he feels."

Yep, just like Luke felt something for Krista, even

though he knew it was inappropriate and wrong on so many levels.

"May I ask you something?" she said.

"Sure."

"Do you really not remember what drove you outside at church?"

"It's a little foggy, why?"

"Because the look in your eye just before you ran out of church was, I don't know, well it spooked me."

That's the look of raw anguish, sweetheart.

"What did I look like?" he said.

She glanced at him, then back at the road. "Like you just found out your mom died."

His gaze drifted out the side window. She'd read it in his eyes, read the heartbreak and agony that followed. Amazing.

"If you want to talk…" She hesitated. "I'm a really good listener."

"I'll bet you are," he whispered. But talking to her, sharing his buried shame would only weaken his ability to protect her.

"It might make you feel better," she prompted.

"I doubt that."

"Try it."

"I remembered something about my mom." Although his mind told him to shut his mouth, his heart couldn't stop the words.

"Is she…?"

"Dead. Passed away when I was fifteen."

"Oh, Luke, I'm so sorry."

"It happens."

A few minutes of silence passed as they drove through the heart of town to get to Krista's house. He thought he was off the hook.

"Do the holidays make you sad because you think of your mom?"

"Has nothing to do with the holidays."

"Then what—"

"I remembered she was a drunk, okay? And all the church people knew about it and pitied me and gave me handouts. I hated it."

"They were trying to help."

"I don't need anybody's help, not now, and I certainly didn't need it then."

"Everyone needs help once in a while, Luke."

"Not me. Don't need it, don't want it."

"Ever?"

"Never."

"But why—"

"Because when I let someone help I get them killed."

FIFTEEN

Krista gripped the steering wheel, shocked by his confession. She knew how she wanted to respond. She wanted to ask him pointed questions about what happened and why he blamed himself for needing someone's help. She suspected it had to do with his partner.

She glanced his way, but his eyes were closed and he was rubbing his temples. He'd shut down. He was in pain, and she should give him space. For now.

They pulled into her driveway and she noticed the kitchen light on. "I don't remember leaving the light on."

He snapped his attention to the house and squinted.

Opening his door, he said, "I'll check it out."

"I'm going with you."

He shot her that look she figured was meant to intimidate her into staying in the car, but she ignored it. There was no way she was letting him walk into a potentially dangerous situation after just being knocked out. She grabbed the plate of food meant for Natalie and followed him.

"Let's get Roscoe to help us out." He went to the

garage and opened the side door. He'd left a lamp on for the dog, only…

…the dog wasn't there.

"Roscoe," she hushed.

"Stay here, got it? No back talk on this one."

She nodded, remorse gripping her chest at the thought that someone had taken or hurt the dog. He closed the garage door and she clicked off the light to watch him approach the house. He crept toward the back door and reached inside his jacket for his gun. She swallowed back her panic, slowed her breathing so she wouldn't pass out.

She wanted this whole thing over, wanted to get back to her uneventful, normal life. She'd collected some good information for Luke tonight at the potluck, and was looking forward to sharing it, yet they hadn't had a chance to talk about it since they'd left church.

Pulling out her phone, she got ready to call 9-1-1.

Roscoe's bark echoed from the house.

"What the…?" she whispered to herself. How did he get inside? The back door opened and Luke holstered his gun. Officer Deanna West stood in the doorway. Luke motioned for Krista to join him.

Krista went to the back door. "Hey, Deanna."

"Hi, Krista. Food for me? Thanks." Her brown eyes widened with anticipation.

"I'd brought it for Natalie, but she's not up for visitors." Krista slid the plate onto the counter.

"More like the ball and chain isn't up for visitors," Deanna added.

"You don't like Timothy?" Luke asked, settling into a kitchen chair.

"He's a wee bit possessive for my taste. Hey, as long as you're here with Krista, I need to run a few errands."

"No problem," Luke said.

"I'll be back in an hour. I've got a key, obviously."

"Where did you—"

"Under the purple pot outside," Deanna interrupted Krista. "Anyone who knows you could figure that out."

"I'm so transparent," Krista said.

"You can say that again," Luke added while petting Roscoe.

"You say it like it's a bad thing," Krista retorted.

"Well, I'll leave you kids to fight." Deanna winked and breezed out the back door.

Krista leaned against the counter. It was nearly nine and she was beat, but she needed to share information with Luke in hopes of helping him solve this case.

"Wanna know what I found out tonight?" she said.

Luke glanced up.

"I heard a few interesting things that may or may not mean anything." She sat down next to him and propped her chin on her upturned palm. "First, someone broke into Luanne Sparks's car two days ago."

"And this is important because…?"

"She went to Mexico with us and hadn't unloaded her souvenirs from the car yet. Her daughter got sick and couldn't watch the twins, so Grandma Luanne had to jump in and while the car was parked outside someone got into the trunk and emptied it out. And I'm sure this is nothing, but Alan bought a hunting rifle a few days ago. He told Ned at the hardware store that he was concerned about the sudden crime wave in Wentworth and needed it to scare off any potential intruders."

"That guy with any kind of gun…" He shook his head.

"Timothy's sheet metal business is going well. He just got a big contract from All Star Roofing, which accounts for his buying property up north. Lucy and Ralph Grimes bought an old farmhouse outside of Muskegon to rehab, and there was one other thing." She paused and tapped her forefinger to her chin. "Oh, Phillip Barton bought a new car."

"That's big news," he said, half kidding.

"It is if the guy runs a boat business. He can't make that much money."

"The chief told me he owns a seat on the board of trade."

"Yeah, but a Mercedes SL?" She shook her head. "Has to cost—"

"They start at around a hundred thousand."

"Who can afford that? And who needs it?"

"Have you ever driven one?"

"Have you?"

"No, but I can imagine it's a pretty nice ride."

She made a face.

"I was going to look into Phillip a little more anyway."

"I'd better warn you, some of the ladies are asking

for your number so when you're done at the tea shop you could to do some 'honey do' chores for them."

"You'd better add to my list."

He seemed less intense for the moment, so she dived in. "I'm taking a guess, but did you ask your partner for help and that's when he was killed?"

Luke leaned back in his chair. "Boy, woman, you switch gears faster than a driver at Indy."

She studied him, wondering if he'd answer. It was a nosy question, sure, but she really felt like she could help him, ease some of the angst twisting him in knots, if she knew more about his situation.

Through the grace of God anything was possible.

"I should have handled it on my own," Luke whispered.

"Handled what?"

"I got a tip, thought I could use backup, so I called Karl. I should have alerted my supervisor. He would have sent a team, but I thought I had it under control." He pinned her with cool, blue eyes. "I didn't."

"And Karl was killed."

Luke slowly tapped his finger on the kitchen table as if calming himself. "He left behind a wife and two-year-old. I have no family. I should have been the one to die."

"But you didn't and you've gone on to catch plenty of criminals."

"Doesn't justify his death."

"Nothing justifies an untimely death of a loved one."

She could barely hear her own voice, and realized she was sinking into her own dark memories.

"I'm sorry," he said, leaning forward and placing his hand over hers. "We've both experienced some pretty ugly things."

"And some beautiful ones as well, don't forget."

"Yeah, like what?"

"The support of the community when Mom and I moved here. Wentworth adopted us, even though frightening rumors preceded us to town. The people here didn't care, and the folks at Peace Church were amazing."

"You were lucky."

"It's not about luck. It's about love. The love of God."

Luke slipped his hand away.

"God forgives and loves you, Luke."

He snapped his gaze to hers and she nearly scooted back at the intensity she read there.

"He couldn't possibly forgive me," Luke said.

"For what happened to your partner?"

"For what I did to my mother."

Krista steeled herself with a prayer. *Jesus, help me listen with an open heart, and offer forgiveness where You surely would.*

"What did you do to your mom?"

"I made her life miserable." He glanced at the floor.

She waited, sensing there was more.

"Always in trouble, getting arrested when I was

thirteen. She said I drove her so crazy she had to drink to stay sane."

"And you believed her?"

Luke glanced up. "She was my mom."

Right, and we all believe our parents, especially at that age.

"What happened to your dad?" she asked.

"Left when I was little." Luke's cell vibrated and he snatched it from his belt. He paced into the living room. "McIntyre."

As the low timbre of his voice drifted into the kitchen, she sighed and touched her silver charm. It all made sense—Luke's self-loathing because he thought he drove away his father and felt responsible for his mother's drinking. That was so cruel to do to a child. Yet he'd survived his upbringing and grew up to be an honorable man who sacrificed his own safety to protect others.

He was a fine human being. He should be proud of himself instead of hearing his mother's words haunt him from the past.

How could she convince him of that?

"You wanted to know if anyone strange came to town and this is pretty strange," Chief Cunningham said.

Three men had checked into the Crocker Hotel on the outskirts of town. They were sharing a room, and specifically asked for a view of the parking lot.

As if they were waiting for someone. Were they Garcia's men?

"Did the clerk give you a description?" Luke asked.

"Thirties, scruffy-lookin', polite. Two of them were wearing cowboy hats. Said they were here for a party."

Garcia owned a number of ranches staffed by cowboys to get the work done.

"I need to go with you," Luke said.

"You sure you're up to it?"

"I'm fine. Send Officer West back to watch over Krista. Better yet, have her take Krista somewhere else for the night, just until we figure this out."

"Good thinking. I'll swing by to pick you up."

"Thanks." Luke ended the call and glanced at the kitchen. The sound of Krista humming drifted into the living room.

For once Luke welcomed bad news. It meant he'd be out investigating instead of sitting in Krista's kitchen letting her do emotional open-heart surgery on him. He still couldn't believe he'd exposed himself like that, that he'd told her about Dad…about Mom.

He figured he was still off kilter from the knock to the head. He straightened. Could his attacker have been one of Garcia's men who'd registered at Crocker Hotel? Waiting for Krista to come out of church so he could take a shot at her?

He went into the kitchen and found Krista repackaging the leftovers from the potluck.

"Who was that?" she asked, casually, as if the call hadn't just interrupted a raw moment for him.

"The chief. He's picking me up and sending Officer West back to take you someplace for the night."

She froze in mid scoop of stuffing. "Why?"

"Three suspicious-looking men rented a room at the Crocker Hotel. The chief wants to check it out."

"So why do you have to go?"

"They could be Garcia's men. I won't let him go into this alone."

"But you were unconscious a few hours ago."

"I'm fine."

"You're limping."

"My ankle's a little sore. No big deal."

She took a step toward him. "It is if you need to run away from the bad guys."

"Krista—"

"You can't go. I won't let you."

"You won't let me?" He smiled, trying to make light of her comment.

"I don't think this is funny."

"It's my job."

"Don't remind me." She turned her back to him and went back to scooping food into a plastic container.

He'd upset her. He didn't mean to. But this job, going out in the late hours and investigating suspects, was part of the deal. It's what drove him, kept him running at high speed.

Then she turned to him, her green eyes misting, and he wasn't sure about anything anymore.

"I will pray for your safety."

"Thanks."

She closed in on him and the room got incredibly small. Unhooking her necklace, she said, "I want you to take this, for luck."

He eyed the silver charm. "I'll be fine. You hold on to it for luck."

Gripping his biceps, she stood on her tiptoes and kissed his cheek.

Goose bumps shot down his arms and he struggled to catch his breath. This was inappropriate for so many reasons, yet he loved the way her lips felt against his cheek.

The back door clicked open. "The chief is—whoa, sorry," Officer West said.

Krista released Luke and rushed past him into the living room. "Good luck!" she called and raced up the stairs.

"Sorry," Officer West said.

Luke went to the door but didn't make eye contact with the cop. "Get her out of here, somewhere safe, I don't care where."

"I will."

He snapped around and pointed his finger, as if to punctuate his order, as if he had something important to add but nothing came out.

"It's okay," Deanna assured. "I'll take care of her."

With a nod, he marched down the back steps to the chief's car.

Ten minutes later Luke and the chief were at the hotel asking questions.

"Did you see them leave?" the chief asked the teen-age clerk.

"Nah, but I've been texting my boyfriend on and off for the past hour."

"Describe the guests," Luke asked.

"Tall, dark and one was actually handsome," she joked.

"Did they speak with an accent?" Luke pushed.

She glanced up, as if thinking. "Yeah, actually the one dude had an accent."

Luke and the chief shared a look.

She shrugged and handed Luke a key.

"Don't text your boyfriend about this, or tell anyone else until we figure out what's going on, got it?" Chief Cunningham said to the girl.

She nibbled her lower lip and glanced away.

"Who did you tell?" the chief said.

"That's what Ryan and I've been texting about. Trying to figure out who these guys are."

"Don't tell him we're here or what we're doing. We wouldn't want any innocent bystanders getting hurt because they showed up to check it out."

"Okay, sure. But I hate lying to Ryan."

Luke snatched her cell phone and turned it off. "Now you're not lying."

She nodded, a little taken aback by Luke's behavior. Didn't surprise him, but he didn't know what else to do.

With a nod, the chief led them outside to room 7.

A part of Luke hoped this was it, that these were the

guys that would put an end to this case and the constant adrenaline flowing through his body because he was afraid Krista would be hurt.

Yet another part of him dreaded the day he'd have to say goodbye to her.

Focus, McIntyre!

They approached the room and Luke motioned for the chief to stand on the other side of the door. Luke calmed his breathing and readied for an assault.

The sound of male laughter filtered through the window. The chief raised an eyebrow and Luke shrugged. Maybe they were killing time before they carried out their assignment.

Luke tapped on the door with the barrel of his gun, but the guys didn't hear him. He banged louder.

The room went silent. A few seconds passed.

"Who is it?" a deep male voice called out.

"Hotel manager."

"What? We're not being that loud."

"Open the door, sir."

Luke readied himself to kick in the door once they cracked it open.

The seconds seemed to drag on for hours.

Ready.

Set.

The door opened.

Luke kicked the door open in the guy's face and charged into the room, gun drawn.

At three guys playing poker and smoking cigars.

"What on earth, man?" said the guy who answered the door. He stumbled back onto the bed, holding his nose.

Two of the men dropped their cards and raised their hands. The third, a big guy in a checked flannel shirt, glared at Luke.

"Edie sent you, didn't she?" flannel shirt said.

"I'm a federal agent. This is the Wentworth police chief. We need to see some I.D."

The three guys sitting at the table pulled out their wallets. They passed them to the chief who glanced at them, then back at the men.

"Looks legit," the chief said.

Luke holstered his gun. "So what's the deal here?"

"Texas hold 'em," a guy said.

"No, I mean why rent the room to play cards?"

"You kidding? You think our wives would let us have a card game at any of our houses? They hate the smoke, the jokes, the whole thing," one of the guys said.

"So we said we were going hunting for the weekend and we rented a room."

"Just one?"

"I rented one, too," the guy with the bloody nose said, raising his hand.

"The three of us checked in together and Dave came later."

"Suzy wouldn't let me go before I bathed the kids," Dave explained.

Unbelievable. Luke just gave a guy a bloody nose and ruined these guys' night of male bonding.

"Why rent a room in Wentworth?" the chief asked.

"It's far enough away from Stillwater that no one would recognize us and report to our wives," Dave said.

"Although now we'll probably be in the paper," the skinny dude added. "Are we going to be arrested?"

Flannel shirt looked at his friend. "For what? Playing cards?"

"You're not going to be arrested. Our mistake," the chief apologized.

"Sorry, guys," Luke said. "We're investigating a case and three guys checking into one hotel room sounded suspicious."

"Well, we'll leave you to your game." The chief nodded to Luke and they left the room.

Luke was embarrassed, sure, and more than a little frustrated. But he'd do whatever was necessary to protect Krista and put an end to Garcia's reign.

Interesting how he was thinking of her first.

"Well, that's a relief," the chief said.

"Not really."

They got into the squad car and the chief glanced at Luke. "Why not?"

"Someone's still after Krista and won't stop until they get what they want."

SIXTEEN

Krista paced Julie Sass's living room, glancing out the window every few minutes hoping for the chief's car to pull up.

"You'd think *you* were the mother of nineteen-year-old twins," Julie said, sipping her tea in an easy chair.

"We should have heard something by now." Krista glanced at Deanna, who doodled in a sketchbook. "Shouldn't we have heard something?"

"I'm sure they'll notify us the minute they know anything."

Krista glanced back outside. A few minutes later she felt Julie's hand on her shoulder and glanced at her friend.

"Oh, sweetheart, you got it bad," Julie said.

Deanna winked at her.

"Stop, both of you." Krista paced to the sofa, sat down and fingered her charm. She wished Luke would have taken it with him.

Julie sat next to her. "Come on, spill it."

"I'm a little anxious."

"And in love?" Julie offered.

Krista squared off at her. "This can't be love, I mean, it's not supposed to feel this way."

"What way?" Deanna prodded.

"Like, like I'm antsy, nervous, something, I don't know."

Deanna smiled and focused on her sketchpad.

"What's so funny?" Krista said.

"You've never been in love before, so it might feel a little uncomfortable," Julie offered.

"I thought it's supposed to feel wonderful and peaceful and…and—"

"It's nerve-wracking," Deanna said.

"And sometimes frustrating," Julie added.

"And chaotic."

"And thrilling."

"And sometimes, confusing," Julie explained. "But I've seen you two together. I recognize that look. On both your faces."

Krista held her friend's gaze. "It's a disaster."

"I'm an expert on disaster," Deanna offered.

"I should have fallen for Alan," Krista said.

Deanna glanced up from her sketchbook. "That would have been a major disaster."

"Look." Julie took Krista's hand. "If it's meant to be, it will work out."

"How do I know this isn't just happening because he's here to protect me?"

"That's true, there's that thing called transference," Deanna said.

"I know you, Krista, probably as well as your mom knows you. This is the real deal."

"Then it's the ultimate disaster because he lives in New York and I live here, and I run a tea shop and he hunts criminals and—"

"Criminals?" Julie questioned.

"And now I've blown his cover."

Deanna stopped drawing and joined the ladies in the living room. "Julie, it's important that you not say anything to anyone about Luke's real reason for being here."

"Which is what?"

"He's working on a case. He's with the DEA."

"Drugs? Here in Wentworth?"

"We're not sure," Deanna said.

"It's my fault." Krista paced back to the window. "It has something to do with my trip to Mexico. They think someone smuggled something into to my things and a drug lord wants to retrieve it." She glanced at Julie. "That's our theory, anyway."

"Oh, Krista, I'm sorry." Julie went to Krista and gave her a hug. "You must be so scared."

"Not really. I've got Luke as my personal protector."

"Handyman at the tea shop, staying in your garage. It all makes sense now."

"Except for the fact I'm falling for him."

"Speaking of which…" Julie nodded at the window. The chief's cruiser pulled into the driveway.

"Please don't tell anyone about what's really going

on," Deanna said, opening the door. "It could put your family in danger."

"I won't," Julie said.

Deanna went to greet the chief and Luke.

Julie turned back to Krista. "What are you going to do about Luke?"

"There's nothing to do. There's no future there."

"Your faith is your strength, Krista. Don't give up on it now."

Krista smiled and hugged her friend. "Thanks."

"What's wrong?" Luke said, approaching Krista.

"I was just getting advice from my big sister," Krista said.

Julie shot Krista a knowing smile.

"You okay?" Luke touched her arm and looked deep into her eyes.

"Yeah, just tired," her voice caught. He cared about her. A lot. She cleared her throat. "What happened at the hotel?"

"I'll tell you on the way home," Luke said.

Home. Her chest tightened. If only that were true, if only she and Luke shared a home.

"Did you three have a nice visit?" the chief said, eyeing them suspiciously. The chief had been married for thirty years. He recognized girl talk when he saw it.

"Very nice," Julie said.

The twins pounded up the steps and raced through the front door. "Why are the cops here?" Tatum asked.

"I'm here to bust you girls on curfew," Chief Cunningham said.

"Hey, I'm nineteen," Tatum said.

"Me, too," Tori said.

"He's teasing, sweetheart," Julie said. "My girls are home. I can go to sleep."

"Thanks for everything," Krista said, envious of Julie's beautiful family.

"Good night, all," the chief said.

Deanna drove Luke and Krista back to the house and made herself comfortable in the guest bedroom upstairs. Luke went through the house and rechecked all the locks, windows, doors, everything.

It seemed like he was stalling.

"Keep Roscoe inside with you tonight. A barking dog can deter someone from breaking in."

"You didn't tell me what happened at the Crocker." She sat at the kitchen table and stretched out her legs.

"We busted up a card game."

"You're kidding."

"Nope. Four guys needing some cave time."

"Cave time?"

"Guys need to retreat into their caves once in a while to get a break from their women."

"You make us sound like shrews."

Luke shrugged. "It's normal, at least that's what my partner used to say."

"You miss him."

"He was a good man."

"So are you."

"Thanks, but…"

"What?"

"Never mind. What's on the agenda for tomorrow?" he asked.

She realized he was keeping her at a distance.

"I have to set up for a reception at the Silver Lake Lighthouse. They're doing a dessert fundraiser."

"Man, this little town is a busy place."

Luke started for the back door, but she jumped up and caught his arm. He stiffened, his eyes growing dark.

"Tonight, when you went to the hotel…I was so worried," she said. "I paced and I fretted and—"

"It's part of the job. It's what I do." He glanced at the floor, breaking eye contact.

"I know that. But what I realized was—"

He pressed his forefinger to her lips. "Don't say it."

She tenderly kissed his finger. He slid his hand down to rest on her shoulder.

"Why not?" she whispered.

"It's impossible."

"Not if you have faith."

He rolled his eyes, and with a hand on his cheek, she made him focus on her. "I have enough for both of us. Trust me, Luke. Trust God."

She leaned forward and kissed him. The subtle vibration of his moan tickled her lips. It was just as she'd remembered, soft and sweet, with a hint of desperation.

She'd never felt so safe, so at peace, as she did in Luke's arms.

Suddenly he broke the kiss and stepped back. She searched his eyes, but he wouldn't look at her.

"We can't." He reached for the back door, but she blocked him.

"Look at me."

He planted his hands to his hips and looked over her shoulder.

"Luke?"

Clenching his jaw, his eyes drifted to meet hers.

"It's okay," she said. "I wanted you to kiss me."

"But I shouldn't have."

"Sure you—"

"Do you want to die, Krista? Because getting close to me will get you killed."

She touched his cheek. He closed his eyes and sighed. A few seconds later, he reached around her to open the door.

"See you tomorrow," he said and walked out to the garage.

She fretted, paced and worried about him.

Three more reasons to add to the list of why Luke shouldn't let this thing with Krista go any farther. Forget the top two reasons, the fact he lived in a big city miles away from here and his violent career was his priority.

Krista had experienced her share of violence. He wouldn't bring more into her life.

He spent part of the day doing legitimate chores upstairs, building bookshelves and organizing supplies. The rest of the time he spent on reviewing suspects and making calls.

Yet he felt no closer to exposing the local contact. He looked over his list: Phillip Barton, Ralph Grimes, Alan and perhaps, yes, he had to accept it, Krista's friend, Natalie. Luke wondered if Natalie was the target of the car accident all along.

The fact was Natalie's financials were a mess. She was in debt up to her eyeballs, in part because of the floundering real estate market and having loaned her fiancé money to keep his business solvent.

Folks on the verge of financial disaster were the easiest targets for people like Garcia.

"Luke?" Krista called upstairs. "We're taking off in twenty minutes."

"Thanks."

He e-mailed his supervisor a request for a more extensive background check on Phillip, Ralph, Alan and Natalie. A deeper look into their backgrounds could turn up more clues, maybe even a direct connection to Garcia.

He packed up his folders, glanced at the newly organized office and a sense of pride washed over him. He liked doing things for Krista.

You've completely lost it, buddy. Shaking his head, he went downstairs. It was time to load up his car with food and supplies for the lighthouse event.

"Krista?" he said, walking into the dining room. The

chairs were flipped onto tables, and the mop lay on the floor as if someone had been interrupted.

He marched into the back and found Timothy, Natalie's fiancé, blocking the back door. "Looking for someone?" the guy said.

"Krista."

"She's outside with Natalie."

Luke started for the door.

"Don't even think about it," Timothy said. "Natalie's doing an intervention."

"Excuse me?"

"To get you out of Krista's life."

"I think that's up to Krista."

"Yeah, well, she's a sweet girl," Timothy said. "Her mom and grandmother protected her most of her life, so she's lacking the skills needed in this situation."

"And what skills are those?"

"To be able to discern friend from enemy."

"I'm not her enemy."

"You're using her as bait for your criminal case."

"How did you—"

"Natalie told me and I confirmed it with the chief."

"The fewer people who know about this, the better chance I have to find the perp."

"Yeah, well, I won't tell anyone." He paused, looked up and shot Luke a sinister smile. "As long as you leave Krista alone."

"It's kind of hard to keep my distance when I'm here to protect her."

"Correction, you're here to solve your case. She just happens to be collateral damage."

"You could be arrested for interfering with a federal investigation."

Timothy took a step toward him. "Well, you should be arrested for messing with that girl's head and making her fall in love with you."

Silence stretched between them. Love? Had Krista said that?

"Natalie is the love of my life and Krista is her best friend," Timothy said. "She's like my sister, so leave her alone."

"I have a job to do."

"You're a selfish jerk out for yourself no matter who gets hurt."

Krista breezed into the back. "Hey, what's going on?"

Neither man spoke.

"Guys?" She glanced from Timothy to Luke.

"Timothy, Nat's really tired. You'd better get going." She gave Timothy a hug and Luke wanted to rip them apart.

Not because Timothy thought of her in a romantic way, but because Luke wanted her depending on Luke, leaning on him, not on this jerk.

She stepped back and patted Timothy's shoulder. "Thanks for bringing Nat over."

"Sure thing." Timothy glanced at Krista. "You take care of yourself."

"I will."

Timothy shot one warning glare at Luke and walked away.

She turned to Luke. "Whoa, what was that about?"

"Not important."

Yet it was very important. Krista's friends were worried about her. Luke actually agreed with Timothy. Krista falling in love with Luke was a disaster with a capital *D*.

"You sure you're okay?" Krista grabbed a box of dishes.

"Yep." Or he would be as soon as he figured out how to stop her from falling in love with him.

Yeah, and how are you going to do that, McIntyre? Especially because he was feeling the pull himself, the pull toward something he'd never felt before.

Love.

Not good. He would have to distance himself from her in every way possible. He'd let things slip, things about Karl, his parents, things that made her feel sorry for him and caused her to have feelings she confused with love. No more. He'd put up the wall and do his job.

Regardless of how he was feeling about the adorable Krista Yates.

"It's going to be perfect," Krista said in a singsong voice.

Luke finished unpacking the last of the teacups and glanced at Krista. The woman was being hunted by drug thugs, yet she still enjoyed the moment and took pleasure in her work. How was that possible?

She eyed him and tipped her head slightly. "You're awfully quiet."

"Got nothing to say."

"Uh, right. Try again. Timothy upset you. What happened?"

"You first. What did you and Natalie talk about?"

"The potluck, her latest real estate sale, the wedding. They've rented Michigan Shores for July of next year."

"She didn't—" he paused "—say anything about me?"

She shrugged.

"She told Timothy I was a federal agent," Luke said.

"Yeah, I heard that." She sprinkled rose petals across the buffet table. "He was freaking out, saying I should stay away from you because you're not good for me. Natalie explained what was going on and why we're—" she hesitated "—together all the time."

"Maybe he's right."

Krista focused on her rose petal display. "What do you mean?"

"About me not being good for you."

She waved him off. "Timothy doesn't even know you."

"Neither do you, Krista."

She straightened. "I disagree."

"I'm here to protect you. Naturally you're going to be drawn to me. It happens all the time."

"Not to me it doesn't."

"Whatever you think is happening—"

"I don't think, I know."

"Krista—"

"I left something in the car," she interrupted, and walked to the spiral staircase leading downstairs.

"Stop. I'll get it." He didn't want her going out there alone.

She handed him her car keys, but didn't make eye contact. "The lighter should be in the front seat. I need it for the candles." She put on latex gloves and placed tea sandwiches on a china plate.

He didn't want to hurt her, but the sooner she stopped this fantasy about she and Luke, the better she'd be. He went outside, scanning the property for danger.

He'd been here for days, yet still wasn't any closer to knowing who hunted Krista and what he wanted. Luke felt like a fool, and wondered if his feelings for Krista were messing with his ability to close this case.

Maybe it was time to bring in someone else to lead the investigation, or at least act as Krista's bodyguard while Luke flushed out the perp. Another agent would have the distance needed to focus on keeping her safe.

His cell vibrated and he noticed he was low on battery. He'd been so distracted by potlucks and random kisses that he forgot to do the most basic things.

"McIntyre," he answered.

"It's Marks. Got prints on the note. You know some-one named Alan Jameson?"

Luke's straightened. Alan was always close to Krista, checking on her, touching her.

"I'll question him as soon as I can," Luke said.

"Anything else you need from us?"

"Don't suppose the suitcase was any help?"

"Haven't got the labs back. I'll call as soon as I do."

"Thanks."

Luke grabbed the lighter from the car and walked back to the lighthouse, waiting for Alan to pop out of the shadows. Luke had a hard time believing he was involved in an international drug ring.

He made his way up the spiral staircase and handed Krista the lighter.

"Thanks."

She smiled, as if they hadn't just argued about their relationship, as if he hadn't just hurt her feelings. But he knew he had. He'd seen it in her green eyes.

"My boss called with a lead," he said.

He hesitated. "And?"

"How well do you really know Alan?"

She pinned him with disbelief in her eyes. "You're kidding me."

"Afraid not."

"Alan is always so nice and solicitous. I guess the whole time he was playing me because he wanted to smuggle drugs?"

"I doubt it's that simple."

She shrugged. He knew she didn't like Alan romantically, but still, she'd developed a certain amount of trust for the man.

Trust now broken.

"I'll call the chief and ask him to bring Alan in for questioning. What's left to do here?"

"I can teach you how to fold napkins," she offered as she lit a candle on the buffet table.

Luke groaned, then pulled out his cell and called the chief with the news about Alan.

Suddenly the lights went out, plunging them into darkness.

SEVENTEEN

Luke grabbed Krista's hand and shifted her behind him. He slipped his other hand inside his jacket and pulled out the Glock, careful not to flash it to Krista.

"Someone forget to pay his light bill?" he joked.

"The wiring is pretty outdated."

They shared a knowing look in the candlelight. This wasn't about old wiring or light bills.

He should check it out, but for all he knew this could be a diversion to get him to leave her alone, unprotected and vulnerable.

"Has this ever happened before?" he asked.

"Once."

"What did you do?"

"Called Luther, the maintenance guy."

"Call him."

"My purse is under the table."

Pointing his gun at the stairs, he led her to the buffet table and she got her cell phone from her purse.

"It's going to voice mail," she said.

"Leave a message. Then call the chief."

She made the calls. "What now?"

"We wait." He didn't have much choice. Once people started arriving, they'd be relatively safe. A crowd would chase off the stalker, if he's what caused this blackout. It could just be a power surge, after all, she had hot pots and soup warmers plugged in.

He scanned the room and spotted an ice chest in the corner. "Let's get behind the ice chest."

Their position behind the wooden icebox shielded them from a frontal assault. Although if there were more than one guy coming up those stairs and they packed more than a typical handgun, Luke was toast.

"It's Garcia's men, isn't it?" Krista asked.

"Maybe, maybe not."

She put trembling hands together in prayer and whispered under her breath. Her prayers seeped into his chest and he found himself wanting to whisper along with her.

But God didn't answer prayers for people like Luke McIntyre.

"…Lord, all-forgiving…" she whispered.

Luke blocked out her voice and focused on the stairs, on the attacker.

But no one came. The lighthouse drifted into an eerie silence.

Krista stopped praying. Seconds slowly ticked by, adrenaline flowing through his body, making his heart race triple time.

"Luke?" she whispered.

"Yeah?" He didn't look at her.

"If we die—"

He glanced at her. "I won't let that happen. Not to you."

"I want you to know I've never felt this strongly about a man, I mean, the way I feel for you."

He redirected his attention to the stairs. "It's transference, Krista. It happens in cases like these."

"Then why do you feel it, too?"

A door slammed downstairs. "Krista?" a male voice called.

"Timothy?" she said, scooting out from behind Luke.

He holstered his gun and accompanied her to the top of the stairs. "Don't go down there."

"It's just Timothy," she said.

"What happened to the lights?" Timothy said, coming up the stairs with a flashlight.

He flashed it in Luke's face, probably to irritate him. "What's going on here?"

"We were setting up and the lights went out," Krista explained. "What are you doing here?"

"Natalie asked me to drop off some brochures for the new property in Millstown. Who were the two guys outside?"

"What guys?" Luke said.

"Two guys hovering by the garage. They saw me and took off."

"Did either of them look familiar, like Alan Jameson?"

"No, they were bigger than Alan."

"Which direction?"

"Toward Alpine Lodge next door."

"Stay with her," Luke said and rushed past Timothy.

"Luke, don't," Krista called after him.

Nothing was going to stop him from pursuing the guys who'd been stalking Krista. He flew down the stairs and out the back door.

He kept flush to the garage, took a deep breath, and eyed Alpine Lodge. Besides the news about Alan, this was the best lead they'd had and he wasn't letting it slip through his fingers.

Keeping low, he sprinted across the property to the lobby and peeked inside. There was a woman behind a desk reading a magazine, but no customers in sight. Luke slipped his gun into his holster and stepped into the lobby.

The middle-aged woman glanced up and smiled. "Hi. What kind of room would you like?"

"Actually, I don't need a room." Luke flashed his I.D. "I'm looking for two guys, husky-looking?"

"Don't have anyone like that staying here."

"Did you see anything strange or unusual outside tonight?"

"It's so dark out, I can hardly see anything but my own reflection in the window. Sorry."

"Who are your guests?"

"You mean all four of them?" she chuckled. "Let's see, Mr. Pete Ingram, in town on business. Wanda and Monroe Casperson, in town visiting their grown kids.

And Lyle Alder." She glanced up. "Traveling salesman on his way to Traverse City."

"You always know so much about your customers?"

"I like them to feel at home." She smiled.

"Okay, well, if you think of anything…" He handed her a card. "Have a good night."

"You, too."

He stepped back outside into the frigid night. Chasing his tail again, yep, that's what he was doing. Round and round, and never catching it.

As he headed back to the lighthouse, a small pickup pulled into the driveway. An older gentleman got out and grabbed a toolbox.

"You Luther?" Luke said.

"Yep. Lost power again, did she?"

"She?"

"Madeline, the house." He pointed.

"Yeah." Okay, so some people named cars, and this guy named houses.

"I'll start with the fuse box," Luther said.

"Mind if I look on?"

"Doesn't bother me."

Flashing lights sparked across the property as the chief pulled up behind the pickup. He swung open the door. "What's going on?"

"Lights went out," Luke said. "Krista's upstairs. Could you check on her?"

With a nod, the chief went into the lighthouse and Luke followed Luther into the basement. Luther flipped the switch for the basement light. It didn't come on.

Luther pointed the flashlight at the fuse box and hummed.

"Easy fix," Luther said. He flipped the fuse switch and lights popped on. "Wish they were all this easy."

Luther headed upstairs. "You comin'?"

"In a minute."

The guy nodded and went upstairs.

Luke glanced at the dirt floor and spotted an orange, foil candy wrapper. He squatted and picked it up, thinking it looked familiar, but he couldn't place where he'd seen it.

So it wasn't a random blown fuse. Someone had purposely shut off the power…to what? Scare Krista? Attack her?

The guy had to assume Luke would be close and because word had gotten out that Luke carried a firearm, the perp would know she'd be protected.

Something was off. A smart perp would go after Krista when she was alone, or at least not with Luke.

He went upstairs where the chief was grilling Krista.

"The lights went out, that's all," she said, glancing at Luke.

That wasn't all. A few minutes ago he'd stopped her from professing her love for him. He knew that's what she was about to say, and he couldn't let her, wouldn't let her say it out loud. Then it would be real, and he'd have to deal with his own feelings.

She was right. This wasn't simple transference.

Timothy placed his hand on Krista's shoulder. "You sure you're okay?"

"I'm fine. And I have to get ready for the reception."

"You call if you need anything," Timothy offered.

"Of course. Love to Natalie."

He kissed her cheek. With a curt nod to Luke, Timothy left.

Krista got busy putting baked goods on a plate.

"Can I talk to you downstairs?" Luke said to the chief.

Krista glanced over her shoulder, but didn't say anything. No, they'd both said enough.

Once downstairs, Luke turned to the chief.

"So it wasn't a random outage?" the chief asked.

"No, sir."

"What are you thinking?"

"That someone knocked the lights out figuring I'd come after them, leaving her alone and giving them access."

"They're like a hound dog sniffing out a trail."

"Timothy saw two guys running toward Alpine Lodge. I spoke to the woman at the desk. She didn't see anyone or anything suspicious."

The chief shook his head. "This is getting stranger and stranger."

"I'm thinking of requesting backup."

"Probably a good idea, for everyone." The chief pursed his lips.

"What do you mean?"

The chief nodded toward the lighthouse. "She's taken to you. It's obvious. And she's gonna get hurt."

"Not intentionally."

"I know that, son, but all the same…"

"I'll have the other agent stick close to her while I finish the investigation."

"Good plan. What's on the schedule for tomorrow?"

"I'm hoping a day off."

"That's right, it's Sunday. Okay, we'll see you at church, then."

Church? He had to be kidding.

As he watched the chief drive off, Luke realized he might not have a choice. If Krista went to church Luke would have to follow her, sit with her…

…pray with her.

Surprisingly, he wasn't turned off by the thought after everything he and Krista had been through these last few days. They'd been lucky so far, Krista hadn't been hurt and somehow he'd been able to protect her.

He had a little help with that. Divine help.

That's when it hit him—he should go to church with Krista if for no other reason than to thank God for allowing him to protect her.

Protect her…and fall in love with her.

It was Sunday, church day. He still couldn't believe he was here, sitting next to Krista in church.

Halfway through the service, the knot in Luke's chest seemed to melt away. He let the music drift over him and released the tension he'd been holding on to for the past few days.

Krista was right. He did feel safe here, accepted in a way he'd never felt before.

Walking into the place hadn't been easy. He'd hesitated at the door.

"There are no enemies here," Krista had whispered and led him inside. She assumed he was scanning the place for suspects, when in fact he was in awe of the atmosphere of Peace Church.

Then again, it had been years since he'd stepped into a church. It had been…

His mother's funeral. The day he'd been completely abandoned. Dad had been gone for years; Grandma Annie and Grandpa Joe had passed away when Luke was young. Luke had been left all alone.

You're never alone, an inner voice whispered.

He glanced up at the colorful stained-glass windows. Oddly, here, in this place, he didn't feel so alone.

Yet deep down he didn't feel that he deserved forgiveness.

Krista squeezed his hand. He glanced into her eyes and was immediately transported into a fantasy of living in Wentworth with her, helping her run the shop, taking Roscoe on walks around Silver Lake.

"Amen," the congregation said.

People gathered their things, the hum of conversation floating in the air.

"See, that wasn't so bad, was it?" she said with a smile.

"No, it wasn't."

"Hey, Krista, Luke," Julie Sass greeted them. "You guys coming to the warming house for caroling after the tree lighting tonight?"

"It's not even Thanksgiving yet," Luke said.

"It's a tourist town. We start the celebration before Thanksgiving to give retailers a bump just before Turkey Day," Julie explained. "So what do you think? Stop by for hot chocolate later? Or did you guys have something else planned?" Julie smiled.

Krista actually blushed and Luke found himself drifting, toying with the possibilities.

"We'll see," Krista said.

"Hey, Krista, they're having problems with the coffeepot again," an older woman said from the back of church.

"Duty calls." She squeezed Luke's hand and headed down the aisle toward the back of the church.

"I can help," he called after her.

She turned. "Stay. I'll be right back."

He was about to follow her, but was flanked by Lucy and Ralph Grimes. He'd scratched them off the suspect list after the background check.

"When can you stop by the farm to do some handiwork?" Lucy asked.

"I didn't know—"

"I can do it," Ralph argued with her.

"You cannot. You should see what this boy has done with Krista's tea shop."

"I asked him first," the streusel lady from the pot-luck said.

"Wow, now you've got them fighting over you," Julie joked.

"Let's go, Lucy." Ralph glanced at Luke. "Nice to see you at church, son."

"You, too."

Son. The chief called him son and Mr. Grimes called him son. And for some reason, Luke didn't mind.

He realized standing here amongst the congregation that he felt a part of something bigger than himself, bigger than the DEA and catching bad guys.

He liked the feeling.

"We'll see you tonight, then?" Julie said.

"Most likely."

"By the way, thanks," she offered.

"For what?"

"Being good to Krista. I've never seen her smile this much."

With a nod, Julie walked away.

Leaving Luke with a whole slew of guilt to process. He was here to protect Krista, but he was also using her for his case, sticking close to get a lead on what Garcia's men were after.

No, that was his original motivation for coming here. Find the bad guy and shut him down.

Things had changed.

As people filed out of church Luke sat back down, taking a second to evaluate the turn of events.

He wasn't just here to close the Garcia case. He was here to protect Krista.

Because he was falling in love with her.

Help me, God, he prayed silently. *I want to do right by her.*

For the first time in forever he wondered, was forgiveness possible? Could he have another chance to live a normal, productive life with a generous and kind woman like Krista?

"Hey," Krista said, sitting next to him.

He glanced at her. "Everything okay with the coffeepot?"

"It's old and stubborn. Sometimes you need to get rid of the old stuff to make way for the new."

"Very true."

She took his hand and held it for a few minutes. He could tell she reveled in the peaceful atmosphere of her church.

"Did you enjoy the service?" she said.

"It wasn't as bad as I thought."

"It was wonderful." She looped her arm through his and glanced out the top windows.

He'd always remember her this way, tipping her face to the light, a slight smile curving her lips. She was sweet and gentle. And perfect.

"Okay, love birds, time to fly out of here," Pastor White said from the back.

"Sorry, Pastor," Krista said, standing.

"Don't be sorry. I'd let you stay longer, but I need to visit Dorothy Greko at the hospital."

Luke and Krista shifted out of the pew and walked up the aisle, still holding hands.

The pastor smiled at them. "See you at the tree lighting?"

"We'll be there." She glanced at Luke and smiled.

"So, what's on the agenda for the rest of your day?" he said.

"Relax, update my blog, pet the cat, if she's still talking to me."

"Cats talk?" he teased, walking her to the car.

"Do they ever."

"I'd like to see that."

"You mean hear it."

"That, too."

He opened the passenger door for her and his cell vibrated. "McIntyre," he answered.

"They lost Garcia's men in Chicago. It's a pretty good bet they're coming your way."

EIGHTEEN

Krista wasn't sure what the phone call was about, but it completely changed Luke's mood from warm and friendly to cool and distant.

He was back in agent mode, continually scanning their surroundings, giving one syllable answers, not engaging in conversation.

She knew what she'd seen in church. Luke had made a connection to God. She read it in his blue eyes as they walked out together, holding hands.

But now, as she sat in her kitchen working on her blog, she could feel his tension from across the room as he stared out the side window, waiting for something or someone.

She wanted the warm and caring Luke back.

"Wanna see the rest my pictures?" she said.

He glanced over his shoulder. "Of what?"

"My mission trip."

He glanced out the window, then back at Krista. "Sure."

She clicked on the slide show of children in

class, attending church service, and the trip to the countryside.

"Was the countryside pretty flat?" he asked.

"Some of it. But there were mountains as well."

A picture flashed on the screen of Krista kneeling beside a group of children.

"You look like a natural with kids," Luke said.

"Thanks."

"What's that?" He pointed to a bright red building in the background.

"I don't know. Some kind of manufacturing plant, I guess."

She clicked through the photos and landed on a little boy with his arm around a little girl's shoulder.

"Cute," he said.

She sighed and leaned back in her chair. "I would have taken more, but two guys were swearing at me in Spanish, telling me to get away from the kids."

"Why? Because you were taking pictures?" Luke squinted to see two guys in the background, one bald, the other with thick, black curly hair.

"I guess. They don't trust us."

Someone tapped on the back door.

"I wasn't expecting anyone," Krista said.

"I am."

He opened the door and the chief stepped into the kitchen. "Krista," he greeted, then eyed Luke. "Want to talk outside?"

"No." Krista stood and planted her hands on her hips.

"You have to stop keeping things from me. It's my life that's in danger."

"I'm trying to protect you," Luke said.

"By keeping me in the dark?"

Luke sighed and glanced at the chief. "Go ahead."

"He wasn't home and no one's seen him."

"Who?" Krista pushed.

"Alan," Luke said.

"Why are you looking for Alan?"

"We found his fingerprints on something at the tea shop," Luke said.

"He's my friend, he's been there a lot. What's the big deal?"

"It was a threatening note. I found it in your office and sent it in."

She shook her head in disbelief. "But why would he... you think he's the local contact for the drug cartel? No, that's not possible."

"His house was locked up tight, lights were off, car was in the garage," the chief said.

"So he hasn't left town."

None of this made sense. Alan was a nice, polite man, always protective of Krista.

"He was our best lead," Luke said.

"What should we do next?" the chief said.

"Tell your officers to be on the lookout for two strangers, guys who work for Garcia."

He thought for a minute, then pinned her with his dark blue eyes. "Do you trust me?"

"Of course."

"Good. We're going to put an end to this. Tonight."

Excitement buzzed in the air as flurries drifted down to coat the branches of the city's official Christmas tree.

Krista clung to Luke's arm, pretending, just for a second, that this moment was real, and not some strategy to expose the bad guys who'd been hounding her since her return from Mexico.

The moment passed when someone bumped into her and she practically launched into Luke's arms for protection.

"You really came!" Julie Sass said, hugging Krista.

"I really did," Krista said.

"Not you." She pointed to Luke. "Him."

Luke smiled, but continued to scan the crowd for danger.

"I don't go anywhere without him," Krista covered for him.

"No, you don't, do you?" With a sad smile, she said, "Well, I'm doing cider, so I'd better scoot. Hey," she said to Luke.

Krista nudged him to pay attention.

"What? Sorry."

"Take care of my friend," Julie said.

"Yes, ma'am, I plan to."

Julie drifted off into the crowd. There must have been a few hundred folks in the town square. It was the biggest thing to happen in Wentworth County besides the summer boat races.

Luke led Krista toward the Christmas tree. "Any advice on the best vantage point?"

"It really doesn't matter. Once the tree's lit, you can see it from anywhere."

They edged their way into the crowd just as the carolers burst into a chorus of "Winter Wonderland." Krista glanced across the square at the shops, lit up and offering cocoa and cookies in hopes of jump-starting the retail season.

As her gaze drifted back to the tree, she spotted a familiar face in the crowd. Timothy.

She waved and smiled.

Timothy glared at Luke and disappeared into the crowd. He was being way too protective of Krista, especially now that he knew Luke was here to protect her, not hurt her.

At least he wouldn't mean to hurt her. But the truth was, he'd leave and she'd be heartbroken.

It was her own fault for falling in love with him.

"What happens next?" she asked.

"What do you mean?"

"We wait for someone to attack me?"

He glanced into her eyes. "No, I'd never put you in that kind of danger. He won't risk doing anything in such a public setting. But once he spots you, he'll follow us to the decoy location at which point he'll be arrested." He tipped her chin up with his bent forefinger. "I'm not going to let anything happen to you, got it?"

"Yep." It's all she could get out. She wanted to keep looking into those blue eyes of his, wanted to make him smile, make him laugh so she could see his eyes sparkle.

He turned back to the crowd, his jaw clenched and his body tight.

This was his job. To protect her, put Garcia's men behind bars and move on to the next assignment.

But tonight she could honestly say there was more to Luke than scouting suspects and nailing the bad guy. Something had changed since that first night she'd met him outside her house.

He had changed since then, gone from emotionally guarded federal agent to considerate man. Maybe he'd changed enough to consider a life with Krista?

"What's wrong?" Luke said, his eyes focused on the crowd.

"Why do you think anything's wrong?"

"You're staring at me."

She snapped her gaze from studying his profile. "I was thinking about…" she hesitated. Did she dare? "If you and I had met under different circumstances."

"Yeah, I know what you mean."

"You do?" She didn't risk looking at him.

"Let's talk about this later, when you're safe."

"Sure, okay." They were going to talk about it? She wanted to do the happy dance right here in the middle of the town square. He was admitting to feeling something for her, right? Admitting that there was *something* to talk about.

"So about my honey-do list," Lucy Grimes said, brushing up against Luke.

"Mrs. Grimes, you are relentless." Luke smiled. "I haven't forgotten about you."

Three more church friends greeted them, Luke plastering a fake smile on his face. He looked like he was in physical pain.

Once they were alone again, she asked, "Is it that hard to be friendly?"

"It is when I'm supposed to be focused on protecting you."

"Oh, right, sorry."

He squeezed her hand and she looked into his eyes. "You never have to be sorry. For anything."

She thought he might kiss her, but he turned his head to continue his search of the crowd.

"Something's off," he muttered.

"What?"

"I'm not sure. Come here, get in front of me."

He shifted her in front of him and wrapped his arms around her waist, interlocking his fingers in front. She closed her eyes and leaned back into his chest. They swayed slightly to the music.

This was heaven on earth, leaning against the man she loved, listening to Christmas songs, and being surrounded by friends in the first of the town's celebration of the birth of Jesus.

She could stay here all night in Luke's arms, rocking, humming, wishing.

She wasn't afraid. She knew in her heart that the Lord

wouldn't have finally brought love into her life only to take Luke away from her.

He needs me, Lord.

She wasn't sure how much time had passed cradled in his arms, but the music stopped and people started moving around.

"Where did you go?" he teased.

"I was dreaming."

"About hot chocolate?" he asked.

About you.

"No, I dreamed about going home and having a cup of lavender-white tea."

"Well, let's make that dream come true, shall we?"

With his arm protectively around her, they walked to the car. Luke glanced over her head into the crowd.

"Anything?" she said.

"No, but that doesn't surprise me. He's probably going to follow us. That's the plan anyway."

They got in the car and pulled away from the festivities. She glanced in the rearview mirror, but didn't see any headlights.

"Nothin'," Luke muttered.

She could tell he really wanted to finish this off tonight because he'd made a promise to Krista.

He'd keep his promise.

Then leave her.

No, she had more faith than that.

"Chief Cunningham, come in, over," the dispatch operator's voice called through a radio the chief had given Luke.

"This is Cunningham, over."

"We've got shots fired at 112 Cherry Street."

Krista sat straight. "That's my house."

NINETEEN

Luke didn't want to take her to the scene of a shooting, but he couldn't let her out of his sight.

"Why would someone shoot up my house?" Krista asked, gripping her down jacket.

"Let's not overreact. It could be the Bender kid shooting off a pellet gun again."

She nodded, but didn't look convinced.

"Is there anyplace I can drop you where you'd feel safe?" he asked.

"I only feel safe with you." She glanced out the window.

"How about—"

"No. I have to stay with you."

He took a deep breath and kept under the 35 speed limit. He didn't want to be the first to respond to the scene of a shooting with Krista in the car. Yet he was anxious to know what had happened.

Krista wasn't home. Why would someone shoot at her house? Or did the perp get inside?

"We'll cruise by your house, but you stay in the car," he ordered.

"Okay."

She didn't fight him this time. She'd surrendered completely to his decisions and it scared him. He liked it better when she fought him, argued and stood her ground. He felt completely responsible for her in a way he hadn't before.

A few minutes later they turned the corner to her house and flashing blue lights lit the street. Two squad cars and an ambulance were parked out front.

Luke pulled up behind a squad car. "Stay here."

He got out and walked around the front of the car. He glanced at Krista and changed his mind about leaving her. He opened her door and offered his hand. "On second thought, I'd better keep you close."

With a nod, she got out of the car and they started up the driveway. The sound of an excited Roscoe barking from the garage echoed through the yard. Two EMTs were treating a man in the back of the ambulance. Luke recognized Alan Jameson as the victim.

A police officer stood guard.

"What happened here?" Luke flashed his badge at the cop.

"Chief said to bring this guy in once they treated his flesh wound."

"Alan?" Krista said, stepping toward him.

Luke put out his arm to block her.

"Why's he being questioned?" Luke asked.

"He took a couple of shots at Officer West."

"What? Alan?" Krista said, shocked.

Alan stared at the ground, ashamed, maybe even dazed.

"Come on." Luke led Krista to the back of the house and they went inside. Officer West and the chief sat at the kitchen table. West's hair was messed up and her hands were shaking.

"I thought it was one of them. How could I know?" she said, staring at her firearm on the table. "I mean, why was he shooting at me?"

"Because he thought you were Krista," Luke offered.

Krista pulled away from him. "Why would Alan shoot me? He—" she paused "—likes me."

"It has nothing to do with like or dislike, Krista. If he's the local contact, his job was to get whatever you brought back from Mexico to the right people in the States."

"Alan can't be a drug dealer. I won't believe it."

"Believe it, Krista." Officer West glanced up from her gun. "He shot out the windows. He thought I was you."

Silence blanketed the room.

A third officer came into the kitchen with a rifle. "It's a pellet gun, sir." He handed it to the chief.

"He was going to kill her with a pellet gun?" Chief Cunningham said in disbelief.

"I need to question him," Luke said. He turned and took Krista's hand. "First, we need to get you someplace safe, a place no one knows about."

"But Alan's in custody."

"And Garcia still has men out there. Chief, any ideas?"

"Everyone knows everyone in this town. If Alan has been working with the two guys, they'd probably know where to look for her."

"Natalie," Krista whispered.

"What about her?" Luke questioned.

"She manages all kinds of property. Maybe she has an empty unit?"

"Give her a call," Luke said.

With a nod, she pulled out her cell phone and went into the living room.

Chief Cunningham tapped his fingers on the kitchen table to get Officer West's attention. She glanced up.

"You okay, West?" he asked.

"Yes, sir."

"I'm going to hold on to this for a few days until we wrap this thing up." He took her gun and she closed her eyes.

Surrendering your firearm was procedure after you shot someone. She had to know that, but still it stung.

Krista wandered back into the room. "Natalie said she's got an open condo unit five miles north of Wentworth."

"Good." Luke glanced at the chief. "Can one of your officers take her to the condo?"

"Officer Sherman can do it. I'll take Alan to the station and you can meet us there."

Luke placed his hand on Krista's shoulder. "It's almost over, sweetheart."

Without warning, she wrapped her arms around him and pressed her cheek against his chest. He didn't return the hug at first, embarrassed to do so in front of the chief and Officer West.

"West, why don't you get your coat and I'll drop you off on the way to the station," the chief said.

With a nod, she grabbed her jacket.

"I'll meet you at the station," the chief said to Luke. He and Officer West left and shut the door.

Luke slipped his arms around Krista's lower back and gently squeezed. "It's okay, honey. Everything's going to be fine."

She looked up at him. "How can it be fine when you'll be gone?"

Luke paced the chief's office as they discussed the best way to interrogate Alan. They had to find out how Alan was involved and, more importantly, what Garcia wanted from Krista.

Unfortunately nothing tied Alan to Garcia's business. Luke had requested a trace history on Alan's phone logs and e-mail account. Nothing popped. There seemed to be no connection between them.

"You've got more experience with this kind of thing," the chief said. "I'll follow your lead."

Luke knew he had to choose his words carefully with Alan, question him in such a way that he'd want to come clean. It had to be to his advantage to turn on his drug boss.

"Let's go," Luke said.

They went into the conference room where Alan was sitting at a table. Luke sat down across from him. Alan stared at his handcuffed hands in his lap.

"Alan, want to tell us why you were shooting at Officer West?" Luke said.

Alan didn't answer.

Luke pounded his fist on the table. Alan jerked and glanced up.

"Why would you try to kill a police officer?" Luke pressed.

"I wasn't. I didn't know—"

"Did Garcia give the order? You were trying to kill Krista, right?"

His eyes widened in horror. "I'd never hurt Krista."

"Why, because you love her? Makes sense, right, Chief? You love someone so you try to kill them? How does that work, Alan?"

"I wasn't trying to kill her."

"Sure you were. Garcia told you to take her out so you could get your hands on whatever it is she brought back with her from Mexico."

"I don't know anyone named Garcia."

"Stop lying and tell us why you tried to kill Krista!"

Alan jumped to his feet. "I wasn't trying to kill her, just scare her!" The chief put his hand on Alan's shoulder and encouraged him to sit down. Alan collapsed in the chair and rested his cuffed hands on the table.

"Scare her?" Luke said. "Why?"

"Because then she'd need me."

"Come again?" Luke leaned back in his chair.

"I couldn't get her to commit to our relationship, so I thought if she saw the value in having me around to protect her…"

"So you broke into her house and tea shop and sent the threatening note?"

"I didn't break into her house. I did some other stuff."

"What other stuff?"

Alan shrugged.

"You've gotta tell us or we're going to assume you were behind everything including running Natalie off the road thinking it was Krista."

Alan glared at Luke. "I left the note with the dead mouse, took a shot at the tea shop and shredded her clothes. That's all. I would never hurt Krista. Not like you." He leaned forward across the table. "I know your type. You'll get what you want from her and leave."

"We're not talking about me. We're talking about you terrorizing Miss Yates."

"She needs me. She needs to be taken care of, but she's so independent she can't accept the love of a nice man. No, she'd rather fall in love with a stranger who's going to break her heart."

Luke glared at Alan. There was truth to his words. Luke shoved that thought way back.

Luke's phone vibrated and he glanced at the caller. It was a text from his boss to call in immediately.

"Excuse me," Luke said. He went into the hall and called in. "Yes, sir?"

"Garcia's men were spotted on a toll exchange in Indiana two hours ago. I'm faxing you their picture so you'll know who you're looking for. What's the fax number there?"

Luke went to the fax in the chief's office and read him the number.

"Backup is on the way," Marks said.

"Thank you, sir."

Luke hung up and the fax came through. He picked up the sheet and remarked that the two men looked familiar: one bald, one with thick, black curly hair.

The men from Krista's photographs.

Photographs she'd been putting up on her blog. Her first blog site had been destroyed. Which meant… Had she somehow taken pictures of Garcia's operation in Mexico? Is that what they wanted from her? Could it be that simple?

The authorities had no idea where the base of operations was, although they knew it was within a hundred-mile radius of Mexicali.

Could it be this whole time they were after her photographs, needing to destroy them? Luke knew she always carried her thumb drive on her keychain, which meant they'd never find it, unless they got their hands on her.

If Alan was telling the truth and he wasn't tied to Garcia, and if this was all about her taking the wrong pictures on her trip…

They were still coming for the thumb drive.

And Krista.

Planning his next move, he glanced at the chief's desk and spotted an orange, foil candy wrapper.

Just like the one he'd found at the lighthouse…at the tea shop when he'd found the dead mouse.

"Everything okay in here, son?" the chief said, standing in the doorway.

Luke eyed the chief. "I don't know, is it?"

The chief couldn't be involved in this. Luke's instincts would have alerted him that the guy was dirty. Then again, Luke had been distracted by a sweet and wonderful woman these past few days.

"I don't think Alan's involved with the drug case." The chief glanced at the fax in Luke's hand. "Those Garcia's men?"

"Yes." Luke shifted back a step and held out the candy wrapper. "Is this yours?"

"Timothy recommended them, said they're the best thing for a sore throat in the winter."

"Timothy, as in Natalie's fiancé?"

"Yeah, why?"

"We've got to get to Krista."

TWENTY

Krista gazed at the snowfall from the living room window of the condo. Snow always reminded her of Christmas, her favorite holiday.

It's almost over.

Luke's words filled her with a kind of dread she'd never felt before. It was the first time in her adult life she'd experienced love, the kind that kept her awake at night thinking about the possibilities. Thinking about Luke.

Yet for Luke this was about getting the bad guy and earning redemption for his partner's death.

"How about tea?" Natalie said from the sofa. She started to get up.

"Hey, hey, you're still recovering." Krista rushed over and sat on the coffee table across from her. "You shouldn't have come with me. You should have stayed home and taken care of yourself."

"Timothy thought it was a good idea. With friends around, you won't feel so scared."

"I'm not scared. Luke said the case is almost over."

"And then…?" Natalie shot her a sympathetic look.

"I get back to my normal life. Yay," she said, half-heartedly.

"I'm sorry."

"You're sorry? For what? It's my fault you were run off the road."

"Don't say that. It wasn't your fault. It was the drug guy's fault, whoever has been after you for the past week."

Frustrated, Krista stood. "But why? They got my luggage, they've broken into my house and business and—"

"How about some tea, ladies?" Timothy said, carrying in a tray with cups and saucers.

"If only I had a boyfriend like you," Krista joked.

"Fiancé," Natalie corrected.

"You have a brother or cousin that you haven't told us about, I hope?" Krista joked.

"Sorry, can't help you out there. But I make a mean cup of chamomile tea." He put the tray down and Natalie reached for a cup.

"Hang on, sweetheart," Timothy said. "That one's Krista's."

"What's the difference?" Natalie eyed them.

They looked the same to Krista.

Timothy kissed Natalie on the forehead. "Yours has an herbal supplement I got at the health food store to help you heal."

Natalie and Krista exchanged smiles.

"He's a keeper," Krista said. She took her tea and sat down. Timothy went back into the kitchen.

Krista sipped her tea. It tasted bitter and she figured he'd steeped it too long.

"So, seriously," Natalie started. "Have you told Luke how you feel?"

"Yes, but he can't think about stuff like that right now."

"Stuff? You're in love with him, Krista. That's important."

"And unfortunate."

"Don't say that. Love is a gift." Natalie shifted back into the cushions and sipped her tea.

"I know. But I have to be a realist. Luke lives in another part of the country and works in a violent career. I couldn't go through my life waiting for that day when a police officer came knocking on my door to tell me someone I loved had been killed."

"Right, I forgot about your dad, sorry. Maybe Luke would quit his job."

"That would never happen. You haven't seen the determined look in his eyes."

"To protect you." Natalie yawned. "I'm sorry. My brain needs oxygen," she joked.

"Go ahead and rest. I'm fine."

"Just for a second." Natalie closed her eyes. Krista took the empty teacup from her hand and placed it on the tray.

Krista closed her eyes as well and drifted into a fantasy about Luke being on the police force, attending community events with her, praying with her in church.

If only they'd met under different circumstances, if he weren't a cop and she didn't have such strong ties to Wentworth.

But all the "if onlys" in the world wouldn't change the fact she'd admitted her feelings for him and he kept pushing her away.

It wasn't meant to be.

A door crashed open and Krista sat up.

"Where is she?" a man shouted.

"Why are you here?" Timothy shouted back.

Krista jumped to her feet as Timothy was dragged into the living room…

By two men she recognized. They were the same guys who yelled at her for taking pictures of the children in Mexico.

They shoved Timothy to the floor.

"*¡Estupido!*" the curly-haired guy shouted.

The bald guy pulled a gun, pointed it at Timothy and glared at Krista. "Where is it?"

Krista put up her hands. "What, what do you want?" Adrenaline racing through her body, all she could think about was Luke. How much she loved him. How her death would destroy him.

"Tell us or I shoot him!" the bald guy threatened.

"Krista, please!" Timothy croaked.

"You have to tell me what it is you're looking for."

The bald guy re-aimed his gun at Natalie's sleeping form.

"Krista!" Timothy shouted.

Krista rushed over to shield Natalie's body. "What do you want?"

"Pictures," the curly-haired guy said. "Where you keep pictures?"

"What pictures?"

"From your Internet site. You took pictures in Mexico. We want them."

Heart racing, Krista grabbed her purse and dug for her keys. "They're on my keychain."

"You lie to us!"

"No! They're—" she grabbed them "—here." She tossed her key chain at the curly-haired guy.

"Show us." He motioned for Krista to join him in the kitchen. The guy had a laptop set up. Krista put the thumb drive in place and scanned the pictures.

"Good." He grabbed the thumb drive, then dragged her back into the living room.

This was it. She was going to die.

She kneeled beside Natalie and placed a hand on her back.

"Stand up," the curly-haired guy ordered Timothy.

Timothy stood and squared off at him.

"Garcia es furioso," he said to Timothy. "You finish. We wait outside."

He handed Timothy the gun.

The floor shifted under Krista's knees with the realization that Timothy was working *with* these men. The two men walked out, leaving Krista, Timothy and Natalie alone. Krista wondered if Timothy had drugged

Natalie's tea because he didn't want her to know about his involvement with the drug cartel.

"Timothy?" Krista stood. "What's going on?"

"I'm sorry, Krista. They weren't supposed to come." He shot her a pleading look. "If only you would have given up the thumb drive."

"Given it up? I didn't know they wanted it. And you… you're involved in this?"

"I needed the money."

"That doesn't justify you breaking the law and…and what, you're going to shoot me?"

"I have to. If I don't, they'll kill Natalie. That's why I took her out of the hospital, because I knew they'd come after her!"

"Timothy, take a deep breath. Listen to how absurd this sounds. You're not a killer. How did you get involved in this?"

"It doesn't matter," he said, clutching the gun.

"It matters to me. My father was killed by a gun and if I'm to die the same way I'd like to know why."

Every bone in her body told her to keep him talking, in hopes of making an ally out of him.

"Why?" she pushed.

"Natalie deserves things, nice things. A big wedding, honeymoon, a second house up north. I took out a loan from a guy and couldn't pay him back. He had ties to Garcia's organization and made me an offer to clear my debt. They paid me to smuggle a drug concentrate into the country through souvenirs."

"That's why they broke into Luanne Sparks's car?"

He didn't answer, just stared at the gun in his hand. "All I had to do was get them and hand them off to Garcia's men in Detroit."

"But I didn't buy any souvenirs," Krista said.

"No, you took pictures." He pinned her with empty, dark eyes. "Pictures that exposed Garcia's base of operations."

"I didn't know that. I took pictures of little kids."

Timothy sighed and glanced at the couch. "Natalie wants kids."

"I know."

He glared at Krista. "But I can't have kids if I'm in prison. I'm sorry, Krista."

Timothy raised the gun. Krista dropped to her knees and put her hands together.

"Dear Lord, forgive Timothy for his actions. He's lost and needs Your guidance."

"Stop talking," Timothy shouted.

"Timothy, put the gun down!" Luke ordered from the doorway.

Surprised, Timothy spun around.

A shot rang out, blasting her eardrums, and Krista hit the floor, body trembling.

"Got him?" Luke said.

"Yeah, I'll call for an ambulance," the chief answered.

Eyes squeezed tight, Krista struggled to breathe, fear clogging her throat.

She could hear Timothy moaning in pain a few feet away from her, but didn't want to open her eyes.

Natalie's loving fiancé had almost killed her.

"Krista," Luke said, placing his hand on her shoulder. "Sweetheart, it's okay. Open your eyes."

She did and saw Luke's bright blue eyes staring back at her. Then she caught sight of his gun and thought she might be sick.

A wave of sadness spread across his face as he shoved his gun out of sight. He helped her up and wrapped his arms around her. "It's over, honey. It's all over."

"Two men…"

"We got 'em."

"From Mexico."

"Garcia sent them to destroy the pictures that Timothy couldn't find."

"Drugs."

"What about them?" He looked into her eyes.

"Drug concentrate smuggled into the country through souvenirs."

"We'll get it. We'll shut them down. Come on." As he led her out of the living room, she glanced at Timothy and a choke-sob caught in her throat. Sadness overwhelmed her for her friend Nat. How could she ever come to terms with her fiancé being a violent criminal?

Through friends, church and plenty of time. Krista knew how it worked. She'd been there herself.

"I'm going to have Officer Sherman take you home," Luke said.

"No." Krista clung to his jacket and looked up into his eyes. "Please, don't go. Luke, I love you."

TWENTY-ONE

It felt like a machete had ripped through his chest.

She loved him. Poor Krista because Luke wasn't worth loving. He wasn't nearly good enough for her.

But as she stood there, pleading green eyes looking up at him, he wanted to surrender, just for a second, and tell her he loved her, too.

It was the truth.

Also true was the fact his life's work was a violent one, and this fragile creature needed someone grounded and safe.

And worthy.

He led her to the patrol car. "Are you up to giving a statement?"

"Stop a second." She hesitated and looked up at him. "I promised myself if I lived through this that I would tell you how I felt. I just bared my soul to you. Don't you have anything to say?"

He glanced at the patrol car. "Like what?"

"How do you feel about what I said?"

"Sad."

"Why?" she hushed, squeezing his hand.

"Because I can't give you what you need, Krista. You're confused right now because you've been through a traumatic experience and you almost died and it would have been my fault."

She framed his face with her warm hands. "I didn't die. You saved me."

"It's my job. And it's that very job that makes this thing between us impossible."

"Then get a new one."

"Krista," he scolded.

"What? You couldn't join a less dangerous branch of law enforcement?"

"This is what I do." He opened the patrol car door.

"Because you're paying a penance."

"Because I'm good at it."

"I'll bet you're good at a lot of things."

"Look, I have to stay focused on the case right now."

She sighed and looked at him with those amazing green eyes. "Do you love me?"

"Yes, Krista, which is why I have to leave."

Krista shifted in the chair beside the chief's desk and signed her statement. It was nearly impossible to hold it together, especially when she knew what was coming next.

Luke loved her.

And he was going to leave.

It made no sense, and her frustration was quickly turning into anger…

…and grief. Gut-wrenching grief that rivaled the pain she felt at the loss of her father.

There had to be something she could do, something she could say to change his mind.

"Hard to believe Timothy was involved in this," Chief Cunningham said. "He was the one who broke into the tea shop and drove Natalie off the road, thinking it was Krista."

"He was trying to kill me, even then?" Krista asked.

"No, he was trying to get your purse so he could figure out where you kept the thumb drive. When he went to the car and saw Natalie, he called emergency right away." Chief Cunningham stood and closed the file. "I wondered how he got to the scene so fast."

"And the first night in my garage?" Krista asked.

"Timothy. Did a search of your house and came up empty. Figured out you weren't home yet, so he went to the garage to shut off your lights. If Luke hadn't shown up he probably would have…" The chief glanced up. "Well, no reason talking about it. This case is closed."

"It will be closed once we charge Garcia. Lucky thing Timothy didn't have time to pass off the concentrate to Garcia's men."

"So, what's next?" the chief asked.

"Since Garcia is an American citizen, we'll get moving on the provisional arrest warrant so they can extradite him back to the States for the murder of my partner."

"And the manufacturing plant?" the chief pressed.

"We have no jurisdiction in Mexico, but we'll make our request through the Office of International Affairs. Then it's up to the local law enforcement in Mexico to take action."

"Your work here is done, then."

"Yes." He didn't look at Krista. He hadn't made eye contact with her since they arrived at the station. It was like they were strangers, and she was just another witness in a federal drug case.

But she knew better.

"Well, I should let you go, then."

The chief left his office and shut the door.

"When do you leave?" Krista asked.

"Tonight."

"So you're running away."

He snapped his gaze to meet hers. "I'm trying to put criminals behind bars."

"At the expense of your own life?"

"It's my job."

"Stop staying that. Your life is worth more than any job."

"My life is my job which is why anything that happened between us is irrelevant."

"It's relevant to me." She stood and reached out, but he stepped away.

"Don't make this harder than it has to be," he said, glancing down. "I've enjoyed our time together, but it's over."

"It doesn't have to be."

"No? How does that look, Krista? Us getting married,

you pacing the floors at night waiting for me to come home? Or worse." He turned his back on her. "Work following me home, some thug figuring out where I live and coming to the house?"

"No, because you'll be in a different line of work."

"Can't happen."

"You're using your job to punish yourself for your partner's death. Let it go, Luke. He wouldn't have wanted you to live this way."

"It's best for everyone."

"Forgive yourself. God forgives you."

He glanced into her eyes and for half a second she saw a flash of understanding, maybe even peace.

His cell vibrated and he snapped it from his belt. "Yes, sir?"

As he spoke to, she guessed, his boss, she knew no words would change his mind. She took off her necklace and clutched it in her palm.

She couldn't make him stay with her, forgive himself or allow himself to love her, but she could send a piece of herself with him.

He turned back to her. "Gotta go."

Don't cry, girl. Don't you dare cry.

"I'm sorry you have to go." She went to him and hugged him tight, slipping the charm into his jacket pocket. "I will pray for your safety." She looked up at him. "And your safe return."

With a sad smile, he kissed her. Soft, sweet and vulnerable. She wanted to hold on, but he gripped her shoulders and broke the kiss.

"Roscoe, I forgot—"

"I've gotten used to him. It's fine."

"You sure, because I can ask the chief—"

"It's fine." Having Roscoe around would remind her how much Luke cared for her.

"Take care of yourself," he said.

"You, too."

He turned and walked to the door.

"God bless you, Luke McIntyre."

He hesitated, opened the door and disappeared out of her life.

TWENTY-TWO

As Krista set the tables for the first of many Christmas teas, she realized that Christmas at the tea shop was her saving grace. Preparing for the event gave her purpose and distracted her from the ache in her chest.

Three weeks had passed without any word from Luke. A part of her didn't expect to ever hear from him again.

But that other part, the idealistic part that believed in love, taunted her with hope. She said special prayers for Luke every night before bed, prayers for his safety and self-forgiveness.

That's all she could do. Well, that and mend her own broken heart.

She'd spent many hours consoling Natalie, trying to make sense of how everything had fallen apart in her friend's life. But it would be months, maybe even years before Nat would fully understand and recover. The man Natalie had given her heart to had been seduced by evil and Natalie had no clue what was going on. How did someone recover from that kind of betrayal? Krista wasn't sure, but she'd do her best to help her friend.

"How many do we got tonight?" Tatum Sass said, strolling into the dining room from the back.

"How many do we have," Krista corrected.

"That, too."

Krista smiled. "Twenty-four."

"We're short on sugar cubes."

"Rats, I meant to stop by the grocery store last night."

"I can go," Tatum offered.

"You sure?"

"No prob. I'll be back." Tatum breezed out.

Krista had been a little off, a little distracted since everything happened. Her friends knew it. They were doing a good job of taking care of her, picking up the slack and checking on Krista.

For the first time in a long time Krista didn't mind being taken care of instead of taking care of others. She didn't see it as people trying to control her or tell her what's best. She understood it was about friends rallying to her side because they loved her. Their love was appreciated, but she wanted another kind of love, a kind of love only Luke McIntyre could give her.

"Stop it," she scolded herself. She had to pick herself up and move on. Twenty-four people were coming for dinner, for crying out loud.

Krista clicked into gear and raced around the shop setting tables, lighting candles and brewing tea.

An hour later Krista carefully set the rose petals on a high tea tower and slid it to the side where one of the girls could grab it.

Except for a stubborn whipped creamer and leaky

faucet, they'd avoided any major catastrophes tonight. The roomful of customers seemed joyful and content as they nibbled tea sandwiches, sipped tea and enjoyed Christmas music.

Suddenly Tatum slid into the kitchen.

"Tatum, no sliding," Krista reminded.

"We've got a problem."

Tori slid in behind her. "A major one."

"What?"

"There's some guy out there with a badge, I think he's with the health department," Tatum said.

"He needs to talk to you," Tori added. "Right now."

"In the middle of an event?"

"He said now," Tori punctuated.

"Fine. Tell him I'll be right out."

The girls disappeared back into the dining room. Krista grabbed her coat thinking maybe she'd convince him to talk code violations outside. She was strict about following the rules and had no idea what could warrant a visit from the health department.

She stepped around the corner into the quiet dining room. All chatter had stopped as the ladies stared at a man standing by the fireplace. It looked like…

Luke turned around and shot her an apologetic smile.

Krista froze, unable to speak or even think straight.

Luke walked over to her and took her hand. "I've missed you."

"I'm having a Christmas fantasy, right?" she said.

"If you are, it's about to get better." He got down on one knee. "Krista Yates, will you be my wife?"

It felt like they were completely alone, no customers, no staff, even the music faded into the background. He pulled out a black box from his pocket and opened it to reveal a beautiful solitaire diamond ring.

"I don't know what to say," she said.

"There's a first," Tatum joked.

"Shh," a customer scolded.

"What do you think?" Luke pressed.

"It's beautiful."

"I mean about my proposal?"

She looked into his warm blue eyes and her heart filled with love. "Of course I'll marry you."

The group of ladies applauded. Luke stood and put the ring on her finger. A little embarrassed, she led him out to the front porch and closed the door.

"I'm—I'm," she stuttered.

"You're the most amazing thing that's happened to me, Krista."

"But your case—"

"The strangest thing happened." He put his arm around her and looked up at the dark sky dotted with stars. "I was at the airport about to board the plane to Mexico when I reached into my pocket for change and instead pulled out this." He opened his palm to reveal her charm. "And that hole in my heart opened up and was filled with something more powerful than anger or revenge." He grazed his thumb across her cheek. "Your love and your love of God brought me back, Krista. It saved me from myself. I never want to spend another day without you in my life."

They kissed and it felt like a dream. He was here, holding her, loving her.

They broke the kiss and she narrowed her eyes at him. "Why did it take you three weeks to find your way back to me?"

"I had to wrap things up at work, put my condo on the market, find a job."

"You quit the agency?"

"I did. You're looking at the new security supervisor for Andmark properties. They run Michigan Shores and a handful of other resorts in the area."

"You're kidding."

"What, you don't think I'm qualified?" he teased.

"No, I mean, how did you do that so fast?"

"I guess I've got friends in high places."

"You mean the chief."

"Him, too."

Meaning Luke had done his share of praying for guidance and help. And it led him back to Wentworth.

To Krista.

She wrapped her arms around him and glanced up at the sky. "Isn't it beautiful?"

Out of the corner of her eye, she could tell he was still looking at her. "It sure is."

* * * * *

Dear Reader,

There's nothing I love more than stories about belonging. Feeling a part of a community, whether it's through church, PTA, or work, is a nurturing and powerful experience.

Two things inspired me to write Luke and Krista's story. The first was my fascination with self-forgiveness, or rather the lack thereof. I've run into many people who walk around carrying big, lead weights of guilt on their shoulders. By the end of *Hidden in Shadows,* Luke was finally ready to let go of his guilt and accept both God and love. I wish this kind of healing for everyone.

Second, although Wentworth is a fictional town, it was inspired by my wonderful days spent at Michillinda Beach Lodge outside Whitehall, Michigan. While vacationing at Michillinda—imagine no TV or Internet!—everyone you passed greeted you with a warm, genuine smile. The week included shuffleboard and tennis tournaments, a campfire sing-along, and a talent show where proud parents watched their children take the spotlight for one special night. We ended each evening with milk and cookies in the lobby, and watched the sun set over Lake Michigan. We were strangers who, for one week, became the closest of friends.

May you be blessed with the gift of community and the grace of the Lord,

Hope White

QUESTIONS FOR DISCUSSION

1. Although Krista has experienced trauma in the past, she's able to draw on her faith to keep her steady. How do you use your faith to get through challenging times?

2. Luke carries a heavy burden because he feels responsible for the death of his partner. Have you known someone who carried a heavy burden of guilt? If so, how can we use our faith to help these people heal?

3. Krista didn't like being smothered by her mom and grandmother, so she became a very independent woman. In some cases can being too independent push people away? Do you think some people use their independence as a defense mechanism? If so, how do you get through the defense mechanism?

4. Luke didn't feel that he was worthy of Krista's love. Do you think self-worth comes from messages we get from family and friends? Or is self-worth something you find through God and your own heart?

5. Krista initially wouldn't allow herself to like Luke because he's in a violent career. Have you known anyone in a violent career? Did that color your opinion of him or her?

6. Krista liked Alan, but didn't consider him as a romantic interest. Do you think God wants us to choose our life partners with our hearts or our minds?

7. Krista could have blamed herself for her father's death but did not. Do you think her faith had anything to do with that? Also, how does family and community help you process through the loss of a loved one?

8. Have you lost someone close to you, and if so, how did you find peace through God's word?

9. Luke is determined to arrest the man who killed his partner. At what point does revenge overshadow duty? Have you ever felt the need for revenge?

10. Growing up, Luke resented the church community's efforts to help him and his mom. Has your church helped a family in need? If so, how do you offer the gift in a way that does not make the receiver feel ashamed?

11. When Krista discovered the identity of the local connection, she challenged his decision to work with the drug dealers. Has anyone in your life made a bad or harmful decision to either themselves or others? If so, how did you challenge them to change, without making them shut down?

12. Luke felt he wasn't worthy of Krista's love. Have you known someone with low or little self-confidence like Luke? If so, how do you help them realize their full potential? Are there passages in the Bible you'd refer to?

LARGER-PRINT BOOKS!

**GET 2 FREE
LARGER-PRINT NOVELS
PLUS 2 FREE
MYSTERY GIFTS**

Love Inspired®
SUSPENSE
RIVETING INSPIRATIONAL ROMANCE

Larger-print novels are now available...

YES! Please send me 2 FREE LARGER-PRINT Love Inspired® Suspense novels and my 2 FREE mystery gifts (gifts are worth about $10). After receiving them, if I don't wish to receive any more books, I can return the shipping statement marked "cancel". If I don't cancel, I will receive 4 brand-new novels every month and be billed just $4.74 per book in the U.S. or $5.24 per book in Canada. That's a saving of over 20% off the cover price. It's quite a bargain! Shipping and handling is just 50¢ per book.* I understand that accepting the 2 free books and gifts places me under no obligation to buy anything. I can always return a shipment and cancel at any time. Even if I never buy another book, the two free books and gifts are mine to keep forever.

110 IDN E5TF 310 IDN E5TR

Name	(PLEASE PRINT)
Address	Apt. #
City	State/Prov.	Zip/Postal Code

Signature (if under 18, a parent or guardian must sign)

Mail to **Steeple Hill Reader Service:**
IN U.S.A.: P.O. Box 1867, Buffalo, NY 14240-1867
IN CANADA: P.O. Box 609, Fort Erie, Ontario L2A 5X3

Not valid for current subscribers to Love Inspired Suspense larger-print books.

**Are you a current subscriber to Love Inspired Suspense books
and want to receive the larger-print edition?
Call 1-800-873-8635 or visit www.morefreebooks.com.**

* Terms and prices subject to change without notice. Prices do not include applicable taxes. Sales tax applicable in N.Y. Canadian residents will be charged applicable provincial taxes and GST. Offer not valid in Quebec. This offer is limited to one order per household. All orders subject to approval. Credit or debit balances in a customer's account(s) may be offset by any other outstanding balance owed or to the customer. Please allow 4 to 6 weeks for delivery. Offer available while quantities last.

Your Privacy: Steeple Hill Books is committed to protecting your privacy. Our Privacy Policy is available online at www.SteepleHill.com or upon request from the Reader Service. From time to time we make our lists of customers available to reputable third parties who may have a product or service of interest to you. If you would prefer we not share your name and address, please check here. ☐

Help us get it right—We strive for accurate, respectful and relevant communications. To clarify or modify your communication preferences, visit us at www.ReaderService.com/consumerschoice.

TYLISLP10